D0044670

The Guns of Parral

**Center Point
Large Print**

Also by Lauran Paine and available from
Center Point Large Print:

Corral Canyon
Gundown
Long Bow
Longhorn Trail

This Large Print Book carries the
Seal of Approval of N.A.V.H.

The Guns
of Parral

LAURAN PAINE

CENTER POINT PUBLISHING
THORNDIKE, MAINE

This Center Point Large Print edition
is published in the year 2010 by arrangement with
Golden West Literary Agency.

The text of this Large Print edition is unabridged.
In other aspects, this book may vary
from the original edition.
Printed in the United States of America
on permanent paper.
Set in 16-point Times New Roman type.

ISBN: 978-1-60285-750-6

Library of Congress Cataloging-in-Publication Data

Paine, Lauran.
  The guns of Parral / Lauran Paine. -- Center Point large print ed.
      p. cm.
  ISBN 978-1-60285-750-6 (lib. bdg. : alk. paper)
  1. Large type books. I. Title.
  PS3566.A34G864 2010
  813'.54—dc22
                                                        2009048593

The Guns of Parral

One

The Red Earth Country

It was an enormous territory of rock upthrusts and miles of rusty soft earth the color of red ochre. It seemed to have very little grass and not even the scrub brush grew tall, but there were piñon trees, twisted, unkempt, pocked by the tiny rocks hurled against them by violent desert winds.

There were arroyos deep enough to conceal a dozen mounted men side by side, and gouged-out places where awesome flashfloods had sent millions of gallons of water on rampages between sundown and sunup.

There was a town to the south and east, probably located just over the gradual lip of a barranca by its founders to protect it from the terrible winds. The roadbed meandered around arroyos and over ribs of exposed rock, past piñons and creosote bush, catclaw and barrel cactus. It could have made a direct run on that distant town. One of the pair of riders sitting in piñon shade looking out where that town was made a remark about that, then tipped down his hat and spat amber at a scurrying horned toad.

He was not a particularly noteworthy man. Neither was his companion. They both had stringy, rough necks, lined and weathered faces, and the kind of steady eyes which did not have to move to miss nothing.

They were well mounted; otherwise, their saddles, bridles, gunbelts and weapons looked as though they had come off a bunkhouse wall; they were scarred, uncared for, battered, the kind of equipment people expected to see rangeriders own.

The man who had spoken shifted slightly and spat again. "This'll be our best night in that town, Hank. I figure we'd ought to make it good. Baths, a decent, hot meal, maybe shoot a little pool, maybe buy a bottle and just set there and rust out a little."

The other horseman turned his deeply set, dark eyes upon his companion. They showed amusement. "You left something out."

"No I didn't," snorted the taller rangeman, "I just hadn't got around to it. We'll find him. I know exactly why they sent us down here. What I'm thinkin' is that after four an' a half weeks on the trail we're entitled to a little relaxation. Directly the folks down yonder'll know who we are and then it'll be different. Like I said, tonight may be our best night in Parral, so let's make it worth remembering."

Hank shrugged, lifted his reins and struck ahead at a dogged walk. They could have taken the stageroad, but this way was closer. When they had a closer view of the town Hank made a little clucking sound. "It's got more to it than I thought, Charley. It's darn near as big as Abilene."

Charley turned a screwed-up face. "Abilene? What are you talking about? Parral isn't any bigger'n Abilene's stockyard district. All those shacks you see out yonder, in back of town—that'll be Mex-town and it don't count."

Hank was interested. He had been on the south desert before, but always over in New Mexico. This was his first time on the south desert in Arizona.

There was very little difference, and as he rode down off the barranca toward the upper end of town he arrived at that conclusion. But Parral had trees, and little green patches where the townspeople grew vegetables. Hank sought, and eventually found, the source of all this life-sustaining water. There was an ancient, crooked *acequia* which divided north of town and went southward out behind Parral on the east and west sides, carrying water to all the buildings. He made a little clucking sound; he and his partner had just come across some of the most deadly, desolate desert on earth and had not seen a single stream or running well, but somewhere down here there was an abundant source of water.

As though this had also impressed his partner, Charley Rivers said, "There always has to be a reason for a town to be where it is. Look at the amount of water in those ditches; there's a hell of a well or something around here, Hank."

They did not go in search of it. They were not down on the south desert to admire creeks or wells, or whatever the source of Parral's abundance was, and besides that, it was getting along toward late afternoon.

They found the roadway and turned southward down it. Behind them that redstone barranca rose like a bulwark cutting off the wind, and also cutting off the northward view. Dead ahead, the town was old and settled, dusty and timeless. Indians had founded it, the Spanish had passed through, riding mules and wearing armour, then the Mexicans, imitating their betters, had arrived to claim everything, and later the gringos had arrived as new owners. Parral had remained unchanged through all of it. Now, however, the native Mexicans lived slightly apart, in what the Americans called "Mex-town" and which in fact was over where the original well and plaza still stood.

The buildings were mostly of adobe with walls three feet thick so that the heat of desert summers could be tempered. The jailhouse was opposite Birch's Emporium, which was the general store, and south of Birch's store was the café.

The liverybarn was at the extreme upper end of

Parral in what oldtimers said had once been the drill ground and headquarters for Mexican lancers.

That was where Hank Trainer and Charley Rivers left their animals to be sluiced off, hayed and grained, then stalled out of the heat, and met an expansive, good-natured old man with salt-and-pepper beard stubble and merry little squinty blue eyes who said his name was Walter Ridgeway, and although now he was a corralyard hostler, he told Charley and Hank that at one time, something like twenty-five years earlier, he had operated a trading barn in Parral.

They were interested. The best thing strangers could do in a new town was strike up at least one worthwhile friendship. They invited Walter Ridgeway to meet them at the saloon, which was slightly south of the corralyard and upon the opposite side of the road, then they sauntered forth to enjoy a meal, while dusk came very gradually to mitigate the daylong heat, and around them the town of Parral seemed to be relaxing, seemed to be easing up or letting down as this day neared its end.

The caféman was a taciturn, unsmiling individual with a genuine talent for cooking. Trainer and Rivers stuffed themselves, complimented the caféman, who eyed them stoically, and said nothing.

Outside, they looked down where the rooming-house was and decided to get rooms before heading for the saloon, and that was the way Fate manipulated people occasionally. They paid the woman who operated the rooming-house for a pair of rooms, and were heading back toward the dilapidated old front porch when gunfire erupted up at the saloon.

Rivers and Trainer halted on the porch gazing up the dusk-shadowed broad roadway. A heavy silence followed the gunfire, and for a long while no one emerged from the saloon. Then two rangemen came out with a limp third man between them. They carried him to a small wooden cottage opposite the harness works and several doors north of the stage company office.

Charley said, "Maybe we better put off that drink until tomorrow."

Hank was watching the upper roadway and ignored his partner's suggestion to say, "Where is the law? Most places I been when there's been a gunfight, the law shows up. I haven't seen anyone go in, up there."

Charley fished for his cut plug, bit off a sliver, cheeked it and pocketed the plug, all without taking his eyes off the north roadway. He expectorated over the porch rail into a geranium bed, then said, "You're right, Hank. You don't suppose they don't have no law down here do you? If they don't, we're likely to be in a hell of a fix."

Hank eased ahead, and Charley followed. They

went up as far as the *juzgado* and walked in. Parral's jailhouse had that subtle atmosphere of emptiness, of abandonment or loneliness, which deserted buildings often had. The cell-room door was ajar; Charley looked down there. There was a small back room, and it was also empty. Across it, a locked door faced the rear alley on the west side of town.

Hank pointed. There were three dusty carbines and a long-barreled shotgun in the wall-rack, locked into place by a heavy chain which went through each trigger-guard.

The desk was dusty too, and had papers lying atop it in disarray. Charley turned very slowly to gaze at his partner as he said, "I'll tell you how it looks to me, Hank. If they got one he hasn't been around for a while."

They returned to the roadway, saw a bright light glowing up in that cottage where those two men had carried that third man, and as Hank sighed and went to work rolling a smoke he said, "What about that night of pleasure you figured we deserved?" He lit up, gazing up and down the quiet, empty roadway. "You want a nightcap?"

They headed for the saloon.

The place was about half full with enough blue smoke hanging about chest level to have been supplied by twice as many patrons, except that the scent was different; what looked like tobacco smoke smelled like gunpowder smoke.

13

There were six or seven men drooping at the bar, as quiet as statues. The barman put aside a sour little damp bar-rag to come down where Rivers and Trainer had bellied up, and look enquiringly at them. Charley Rivers asked for two jolt glasses and a bottle, waited until the barman had departed, then slowly turned and considered the men along the bar, other men at tables around the big old gloomy room, and finally completed his turn facing Hank Trainer. When their bottle arrived they took it and the glasses to an empty table over near the front wall along the southern end of the big old room, and got comfortable where they could see the doorway, the bar, and most of the room in other directions.

Except for the silence and the blackpowder scent, it would not have been reasonable to think there had been a gunfight in this place. But there had been, and someone had been hurt badly enough to be carried out.

Hank filled two little glasses, shoved one in front of his partner, lifted his own glass and softly said, "With all that gunfire there should have been another one."

"Maybe they already dragged him out back. Or maybe he's one of those rangeriders up along the north end of the bar."

Charley had been studying the patrons. He had decided those stockmen who were leaning close up there, away from everyone else as though they chose to be aloof or separate, quite possibly had someone among them who had been part of that fight. Charley's reason was elemental; one of those rangemen had his six-gun lying loose in its holster. All the guns of his companions still had their tie-downs in place.

He mentioned this, and Hank shoved out his legs, eased back in the old chair and slumped while he made a study of the rangemen.

He was still doing this when the rangemen murmured among themselves, backed clear to look around the room, then walked out of the saloon with that large man whose tie-down had been yanked loose, in the drag. He was the last one out and he turned in the doorway to cast a sulphurous glance around. No one said a word, or moved, or made a sound. The big man sneered, stepped back and disappeared out into the night.

Two
The Wrong Foot, Again

Hank and Charley exchanged a look, but that was all. Later, however, when they were outside in the pleasant, star-filled night Hank jutted his chin in the direction of the lighted cottage and said, "It's not my nature to butt in where I got no business." He stepped off the plankwalk, and Charley followed after, wearing a rueful expression.

The man who answered their knock on the cottage door was large, stooped, as heavy as a bear, and unsmiling as he studied Trainer and Rivers from the light streaming past from inside.

Hank offered a very disarming smile. "M'name's Trainer. My partner's name is Charley Rivers. We wondered how that feller is making out, the one who had a little trouble at the saloon."

The large, older man continued to stand there, head thrust forward, heavy-lidded tan eyes fixed upon Hank, and said nothing for a long while. Not until Charley shrugged from his position behind Hank and muttered, "Hell, if you're busy, mister, we'll look in another time," then started to turn away.

The big old man growled at them. "He's not in

very good shape. If you saw what happened you'll understand why he isn't. And if you ride for Balinger you can carry word back to the ranch that Cartwright did a good job of it—Jim Hatfield won't be on the range for whatever is left of the season."

Hank smiled at the big old man. "You'll be the doctor?"

The big old man's thick brows dropped slightly and his tan eyes clouded a little. "I'm the doctor," he replied. "Joe Gregg, M.D. And if you didn't know that, you're strangers."

Hank nodded, still smiling. "Just rode into Parral today, Doctor Gregg. About the feller you called Hatfield—my partner and me are kind of nosy—we didn't see it, but we heard the gunfire and saw some fellers fetch someone over here to your house, and we went over to the jailhouse to see if the sheriff or constable, or whatever you got in Parral, was goin' to do anything—and there wasn't anyone at the jailhouse. Didn't appear there had been for a spell."

Doctor Gregg drew forth a huge handkerchief and wiped his hands as he said, "Come inside." He stowed the handkerchief and closed the street door, then wagged his head at Rivers and Trainer. "You are more than nosy, you're foolish. If you don't know what happened at the saloon I'll tell you: Balinger ranch wants young Hatfield to stop fencing. Frank Cartwright is Balinger's range-

17

boss and he's told Jim to stop stringing that wire a dozen times. Jim goes right on stringing it. Today they were both in the saloon at the same time. Well, it was certainly going to happen. If I knew that, then so did everyone else around the countryside, because I'm the last to hear most of the rumors and the gossip."

Charley drew forth his plug, gnawed off a cud, pouched it and eyed the large, older man. "What is he fencing?"

"A wet section he owns. There are not many springs in the Parral countryside. Hatfield inherited ten sections—ten square miles of range—from his grandpaw who died two, three years ago. Jim decided to run a few head of cattle, something his grandfather had never been able to do because Balinger cattle lived all summer off that wet section. You need to know any more?"

Charley wagged his head, shot a sidelong look at Hank, then said, "Doctor, did you ever know a man around Parral by the name of Peter Harkness?"

Joe Gregg went to a sagging sofa and dropped down. He studied Charley a while, then switched his beetling attention to Hank Trainer, and when he spoke he was back looking at Charley again. "Yes, I knew Pete Harkness. If you'd asked me, or anyone else in Parral, that question a year or so back, we all would have lied to you." Doctor

18

Gregg leaned back. "Now it's my turn to ask a question. Who are you?"

Hank was smiling his congenial, disarming smile again. "Fellers passing through."

"Sure you are," murmured the big man and heaved around to get enough leverage to pitch his large, massive body up out of the enveloping old sofa. "Good night, gents," he said, and shouldered past to open the street side door for them. "I've been working hard all day and I'm dog-tired."

Neither of his visitors stirred. They both watched him with interest, and Charley said, "About Pete Harkness, Doctor."

Joe Gregg was in his late sixties or early seventies. At one time, perhaps forty years earlier, he had been powerful enough to go bear hunting with a switch. He could not have been as powerful a man now as he had been then, but men, even old men, never believe that. Never. So Joe Gregg stepped clear of the door and started toward Charley Rivers, who was several inches taller than Hank Trainer, but was also easily fifteen pounds lighter.

Hank gave his partner a sidewards push, and kept pushing him around to the left until they had half circled the big old man and were near the door. Charley did not resist; he had seen the look in the doctor's eyes too.

Hank tried his smile again as he fumbled with

19

the doorlatch. "You've been mighty helpful, Doctor, and we're right obliged. Good night!"

Outside on the porch again with Hank clutching Charley's arm as he forcefully guided Rivers past the broken picket gate to the roadway, Hank said, "They have a lot of disagreeable people in this town."

They returned to the saloon, which had only a handful of customers, and one of them, a stocky, merry-eyed man with white whiskers, saw them and called a greeting. He also told the barman to set up a bottle and glasses, then, as Hank and Charley sidled up, the liverybarn hostler named Walt Ridgeway reminded them that they had invited him to meet them at the saloon tonight.

They filled Walt's glass twice, then took Walt, the bottle and their glasses to that same distant table they had favored earlier, and as soon as Walt had a cigarette manufactured and lighted, Charley leaned on the table and asked Walt if he knew about the shooting of Jim Hatfield tonight by the Balinger ranch foreman, Frank Cartwright.

Walt knew; everyone in town knew and by morning everyone in the outlying cow outfits and horse camps would know.

Charley refilled Walt's glass. "I guess Doc Gregg is fond of Jim Hatfield. We talked to him a while ago and he sure got mad over the shooting."

Walt Ridgeway downed his jolt, blinked a couple of times and said, "Naw. You must have misunderstood Doc Gregg. He don't care for Hatfield. Hardly anyone does. He's a miserable son of a bitch. Maybe we'd ought to have a refill, gents."

They primed Walter Ridgeway until two-thirds of the bottle was gone, and he still had that merry twinkle in his eye. He told them all he knew about Hatfield, Frank Cartwright, even old John Balinger who owned all the good grassland in the Parral territory. He touched upon Joe Gregg—who had been a Confederate during the war—and the barman who was sourly eyeing them because he wanted to lock up for the night: he had once been locked up for horse-stealing.

The only time Walter Ridgeway had no answer to their questions was when they asked him about Peter Harkness. Walt lit a smoke, peered sharply through the rising blue haze, and smiled with his whiskered lips but not his blue eyes.

"You fellers been right decent to me," he told them. "It's been a 'coon's age since anyone's been as decent to old Walt Ridgeway as you boys has." He paused and broadly smiled across the table at them. "For that reason I'm goin' to do you fellers a favor. Don't go around askin' questions about Pete Harkness. Remember that, gents—don't try to bait folks into talkin' about Pete Harkness." Walt arose, eyes twinkling. "I'm real obliged to you. Good night."

As soon as Walt had departed the barman removed his apron, rolled it, pitched it under the backbar and came around his bar at the lower end wearing an expression of frayed patience.

Hank and Charley watched the barman measure the bottle with his fingers, and ponied up what he announced that they owed him.

Outside again, with a slumbering town around them, very few lamps burning anywhere, and the warmth beginning to leave, Hank said, "I think you were right out yonder. This was supposed to be our best night in Parral. We got some folks mad, or curious, or suspicious. From now on—" Hank heaved a mighty yawn and went trudging southward toward the rooming-house.

A distinct benefit of the south desert country— Parral was not on the *real* south desert, it was on the northern fringe of it—was that most of the nights were pleasant, except for July, August and September, and this was early spring. Trainer and Rivers slept like logs, but then, they had also been in the saddle for a lot of hours the previous day, and for a number of days before that.

In the morning they were at the café as its proprietor was firing up his stove. He looked out to see who had come in, recognized that pair of down-at-the-heel rangeriders who had been in late yesterday, and went back to mixing batter and sifting fresh grounds over the older coffee, doing a number of little ritual things, and did not go out to take a breakfast order until he had heard the street side door open and close twice more.

Hank eyed the caféman without great warmth. Normally Hank was a very easy-going individual. Far more tactful and better natured than Charley. But he had been smelling boiling coffee for a while now, knew the caféman was aware that he and Charley had entered almost a quarter of an hour ago, so when the caféman stopped at a tousle-headed, powerfully muscled younger man, a blacksmith's helper in Parral, and asked what the blacksmith wanted for breakfast, Hank arose without a word, went up where the caféman was standing with the counter between them, and said, "You miserable son of a bitch, I'm goin' to time you and if you don't have our coffee down the counter in three minutes. I'm goin' to break your hands, then I'm goin' to break your feet."

The blacksmith's helper looked up in astonishment. So did the caféman. A pair of freighters, big burly bearded men in frazzled old flannel shirts stared at Hank, at the gun he wore, at Charley Rivers who was apparently Hank's friend, and although it was the nature of freighters to be disagreeable, these two settled at the counter and became interested in some prolapsed pies under a big glass dome behind the counter at the pie table.

The coffee arrived with a minute to squander, and as near the caféman came to showing hostility was to glower at the countertop.

Hank reached for his cup. "Two platters of food, cook, plenty of spuds, some light brown toast." Hank paused, and the caféman's curiosity caused him to raise his eyes, which was what Hank had baited him for. Hank smiled. "Within ten minutes, an' before anyone else gets fed, since my partner and I've been waitin' longest."

The caféman's color brightened, his eyes flamed. He was balancing upon the raw edge of violence, and everyone in the café knew it. The massively muscled blacksmith broke the spell by saying, "Glen, leave it be. What the hell, it's only a couple of rangemen."

The caféman loosened a little, then turned and stamped out of sight into his kitchen, and the blacksmith gazed without friendliness, but without open hostility either, at Rivers and Trainer. He could have crushed their skulls; he weighed at least two hundred and ten pounds and there was not an ounce of tallow on him anywhere. Also, he was probably in his mid-twenties, which was something like twenty years younger than the men he was solemnly gazing at.

But they were armed and the blacksmith was not. Charley said, "We was in here almost a half-hour ago, mister. He looked out and saw us.

Since then we been waiting. Would you like bein' treated like that?"

The massive younger man let go a long sigh. "Well, he's got a sort of unusual disposition. Around here, we all know that and sort of put up with it. His brother got killed about a week back. They was pretty close." Hank looked up when the caféman came along with two platters of food, could not catch the caféman's eye, and after the caféman stamped back to his cooking area and Hank sat gazing at the meal, one of those gruff freighters pulled a lopsided smile and said, "They got lots of arsenic in these desert towns—for poisonin' coyotes of course, but still and all—"

His partner snickered and a pair of local men upon the far side of the blacksmith's helper grinned at the wall across the counter from them.

Charley went to work with both hands. He already knew how well the caféman could prepare a meal.

Outside, sunlight appeared abruptly over the building tops and filled the land with a variety of light which could make other colors brighter, more intense, than they could ever have been by themselves, and over everything there was that red-ochre reflection, like ancient, powdered or dusted blood.

Three
A Horseback Ride

The child who handed Hank the note and who scarcely missed a step as he did that, then continued on southward down the early morning sidewalk, could not have been more than nine years of age, and his sudden appearance and abrupt action left Hank and Charley with no clear idea of what the lad looked like.

As they watched, the youth ducked down a dog-trot between two buildings and disappeared. Hank dropped his smoke and unfolded the scrap of paper. The message was brief; Joe Gregg wanted to see them as soon as they had finished breakfast.

They had finished; in fact they were out front of the café at the moment the child had handed Hank Doctor Gregg's summons. Hank handed the note to Charley, who read it and handed it back.

They crossed over and hiked northward as far as the sturdy picket fence with the dilapidated gate, and as they clumped across the porch Joe Gregg opened the door as though he might have been watching out a front-wall window.

As he closed the door and the smell of disinfectant mixed with fresh coffee replaced the fresh air outside, Joe Gregg said, "Hatfield would like to see you gents. I told him a couple of transient rangemen had been around asking how he was. Now he'd like to see you."

Charley scowled at Joe Gregg. "Why, what's he want to see us for?"

Instead of answering the medical practitioner turned and led off at a lumbering, bear-shag sort of walk. He left Hank with the impression he either did not approve of the partners, his patient summoning them, or maybe he did not like his patient and then again it may just have been too early in the morning for Joe Gregg. Many men did not feel nor act human just as the sun was rising.

Jim Hatfield was in a small room where the blinds had been closed. The bed took up easily two-thirds of the room. He was a youngish man, possibly in his late twenties. He had a narrow skull, elongated at the back, reddish hair, and a pair of grey eyes which were ordinarily brighter than they looked now.

He gazed at Rivers and Trainer, listened to what the doctor had to say about these two being the same ones who had been solicitous last night, then made a slight gesture with one hand which was lying atop the blankets. He had almost no color in his cheeks, his eyes had a rather dull look, and when he spoke his voice dragged.

"Doc said he figured you fellers might be drifters—might be looking for work."

Hank stroked his jaw while studying the wounded man. They had not been looking for work, they had been looking for information. Before he could speak Charley was smiling down at the ill man and talking.

"We could use the work, friend, providin' it's with livestock."

Jim Hatfield feebly rolled his head and met Doctor Gregg's glance. He may have nodded, but if so Charley did not see him do it. Joe Gregg gruffly spoke and led the way back out toward the front of the cottage, which was a parlor as well as a waiting-room.

"He'll pay going wages, and to reach the ranch you ride north a mile from town, then three miles due east. You'll find an old set of wagon ruts. They lead to his place, and they also lead on past a few miles to an adjoining ranch, but your only concern will be the Hatfield place."

Doctor Gregg paused, gazing at the rangemen a moment, perhaps waiting for one of them to speak.

They did not say anything, but as Joe Gregg fidgeted a little self-consciously, Charley very slowly turned to catch his partner's eye. Gregg, with misgivings about the purpose of that look, started speaking again.

"You could do a lot worse, especially down on

28

the desert this time of year. All he expects is that you look after things for a while, until he can look after them himself."

Charley finally spoke. "We'll talk about it, Doctor. Maybe we'll ride out there and see what it'll take."

Joe Gregg probably wished for a more definite answer than that, but as the pair of strangers prepared to depart from his house he did not press an issue he was confident would suffer from pressing. Doctor Gregg was a knowledgeable individual; this was his second encounter with Rivers and Trainer, and he had made some shrewd observations about them.

They strolled up into tree-shade out front of the liverybarn before discussing Hatfield's offer. It had one advantage. It would provide them with an excuse for remaining in the Parral countryside. It also had a particular disadvantage. It would isolate them out on some red-rock cow outfit which had no cows on it.

They got their horses from Walt Ridgeway, who was as merry as ever and showed no effects at all from the amount of whiskey he had consumed last night, and left town up the crooked, dusty stageroad before the sun was high enough to cause discomfort.

Hank looped his reins, tipped down his hat and went to work rolling a smoke as he said, "Joe Gregg never did tell us what happened to Jim Hatfield."

Charley turned a creased forehead. "He sure as hell did. He told us that a feller named Cartwright shot Hatfield over—"

"What I mean is, he didn't tell us how shot up Hatfield is," stated Hank, lighting up and trailing blue tobacco smoke in the airless, still and deeply silent morning. "Lookin' at him lyin' in that bed and all—he didn't look to me like he could pull a pup off a green hide."

Charley relaxed and gazed over the countryside, and when they reached the right-side turnoff and left the main road, he said, "Why in the hell would anyone want to ranch in country like this? Why hell, I've seen better cattle country up in Denver City where they paved every darned roadway."

They loped; it was cool and pleasant, the horses could use a little exercise, and the countryside was interesting. It was not all red soil; there were streaks where the earth looked almost fit to farm, but there was one thing both the good and bad land shared—a lack of water.

They found bunchgrass, usually hiding under some kind of desert bush, and the clumps were a fair distance apart. By the time they had buildings and rooftops in sight Charley was wagging his head. "They'd ought to give it back to the Messicans. Look at that, for Chris'sake—only thing a man could raise out here is goats."

He was correct, but a mile east of the

coachroad a subtle change began to occur. There were still streaks of red soil mixed with something like tan adobe, and there was much more grass, increasingly so as the two horsemen continued toward the set of ranch buildings off on their left where the road began to veer right, began to move deliberately away from those buildings and go meandering around the rolling countryside south, and again, southeasterly. It was better land out here. It still would not have put a Montanan or a Coloradan into ecstasy, but for south desert territory it was indeed worthwhile.

They turned in at the set of buildings, and a pair of pudding-footed big harness horses nickered to them from a corral out behind the barn. Otherwise, there was no greeting. Charley was leaning to dismount at the tie-rack in front of the barn when he said, "I guess Hatfield don't like dogs."

It was a reasonable thing to think; no dog had come out to menace them. Very few ranches did not have at least one dog around the home-place, they were almost indispensable.

Hank dismounted, loosened his cinch and removed his gloves, ready to lead his horse inside the barn to be stripped, stalled and fed when a faint sound reached him down the south side of the barn. He looked at Charley, but evidently Rivers had heard nothing. Hank hesitated, then grumbled, looped his reins at the rack and strode over to the side of the barn, stepped clear and peered.

For a moment he was silent and motionless then he called Charley. "Here's your dog. Come have a look."

Charley was ready to take his horse into the barn and was not very interested. He said, "I've seen dogs before."

Hank still had not moved. "Come look!" he snarled.

Charley's head came up and around, he considered Trainer's stance for a moment, then flung back his reins and hiked out there.

The dog was not young; he was not old either, but he had not been a pup in a while. He was lying against the barn with red dust over his hide. He had been hurled against the barn, had managed over the hours to struggle to get most of his body straightened around, but his eyes were sunken and bloodshot. The ground beneath him was clotted with blood, and he looked at the pair of strangers without attempting to move or make a sound.

They went down there, Hank knelt to straighten the stiff, cold legs as best he could, and Charley went out back to a stone trough to fill his hat with water and return. As he was kneeling, supporting the dog so that he could drink, Hank raised a hand which had dark blood on it, and scowled. "He hasn't been shot, but he's sure been manhandled someway. There are some busted ribs and he can't move his hind end very well."

Charley waited, watching the dog lap water; and when the shaking head sagged and Charley put his hat aside to help the dog lower himself, he said, "They got wolves or mountain lions in this country?"

Hank scoffed. "No. What are you talkin' about? If he'd tangled with somethin' like that, his ears would be torn and he'd have ripped places all over his hide."

"All right. Then what did he tangle with, partner, because he sure as hell come off second best with something. Let's get him inside the barn; it's goin' to get hot out here directly."

They were very careful the way they lifted the dog and carried him to the barn. They made him a soft pallet of old blankets and straw, rustled up a big old dented pan for more water, and watched as the animal's dry nose began to show moisture.

They brought their horses inside too, stalled them, and hayed them from a low loft, then went back to the dog and used a couple of old rags they found in the harness-room to sluice him off and bathe his face. He feebly licked Charley's hand, and Charley smiled, lay a rough palm upon the dog's head, and left it there for a moment.

Hank went to the wide, low barn opening

toward the yard and leaned there studying the land, the flawless turquoise sky and spoke almost casually over his shoulder.

"There was riders here last night. They left tracks where they came in and where they rode out. Charley, if I was a betting man I'd say someone tried to kick that dog to death and darned near got it done."

Rivers walked forward and also halted in the opening to study the ground, but he required more than just a cursory look so he walked forth, quartering back and forth until Hank grinned because Charley put him in mind of a bird-dog.

The tracks were there, no question about that, but they were incomplete. Hank led the way over to the house, which was half adobe and half log, and which had been built by someone with defense in mind; there was nothing growing within a hundred yards in any direction, each of the four walls had one recessed window, and when they stepped up onto the ramada and faced the door, they saw the loopholes. Charley made a small clucking sound. "Mister Hatfield is not a trustin' man, Hank."

"If he built the place," stated Trainer and tried the door. It opened inward. "But this is an old house, Charley. I'd say whoever built it did so before Hatfield was out of three-cornered britches."

Hank stepped inside. There was the usual

aroma of old cooking. There was also a dark gloom which was only partially dispelled by having the door opened. Charley went around yanking back blankets which had been draped over the front-wall windows, then he turned to speak, but did not utter a sound.

The room was a shambles. Furniture had been heaved violently against the walls, pictures which had been hanging near the door had been hurled to the floor, papers were scattered everywhere, someone had grasped an old buffalo rifle by the barrel and had swung the stock against the redrock fascia of the old fireplace, completely destroying the gun.

It was not the devastation which held Hank and Charley motionless as they took it all in, it was the obvious, savage violence with which the ruin had been accomplished. Hank finally blew out a long breath and said, "Charley, the dog was lucky. Whoever this feller was. Last night would have been a bad time to meet him."

They went through the five individual rooms and found an identical devastation in each one. In the kitchen, which normally would not be expected to inspire frenzied wrath in someone, the place was a complete shambles.

Charley went around yanking blankets away from windows so a full assessment of damage could be made. Hank finished his examination and returned to the front porch to roll and light a smoke. Charley eventually joined him out there, wagging his head, and Hank put a solemn look upon his partner.

"Would Gregg ask us to live out here until Hatfield gets back because he knows there's someone out to kill Hatfield?"

Charley was whittling a chew of his cut plug and leaning on a porch upright when he answered. "I got no idea, but I'll give you odds Hatfield knows something." Charley got his tobacco nested properly and looked around at Trainer. "Y'know, if Hatfield's got a crazy bastard for an enemy, well, I guess we can clean up the house—but that dog out there. Hank, what kind of a person does a thing like that?"

"I don't know. You want to hire on?"

Charley spat, looked in the direction of the barn and inclined his head. "Yeah, I think I do."

Four
The Return to Town

It required the entire day to get that house back in order, and because there was so much breakage much had to be hauled out to a barrel on the rear porch.

They took time out to eat, and to carry food down to the dog, but he would not eat. He would lie there, sunken eyes showing that he recognized them, and he would feebly wag his tail but he would not eat.

They took him to the house and made another pallet in the kitchen for him, and they spoke hopefully, but neither one of them was really very hopeful.

They went out in the late afternoon to fork-feed those big harness horses in the rear corral, and returned to the barn to care for their own animals. They intended to turn their horses into one of those big corrals out behind the barn in the morning.

A couple of hours before sunset several horsemen loped past a mile or so beyond the yard to the southwest. Charley surmised they would be heading for town, and Hank simply watched. Afterwards, with nothing but a lazy little runnel of dust to show that there had been horsemen out there, Hank said, "Suppose we saddle up and poke around."

They left the yard, riding eastward, and on a slightly southward course, found the tracks left by those rangemen they had seen earlier, and turned down still farther until they reached the roadway, and swung to their left to get some idea where the road went.

There was a lot of country west, north and east of the Hatfield place. It was generally more or less flat but there was an occasional hill. From one of these, several miles from the Hatfield place, they got a distant look at that outfit Joe Gregg had said neighboured up with Jim Hatfield's place.

It was large; they could tell from the number of distant buildings, the size of the yard, the spidery network of corrals, and they guessed this was the place those rangemen had been riding from earlier, the ones they had seen loping toward Parral, or at least in the direction of Parral.

They turned back with the heat making a haze over the southerly desert, and with a metallic taste in the air, as though it might rain, except that neither of them expected that to happen, not down in this country.

They reached the yard, put up their horses, did the chores and went up to the house for supper. Charley thought it might be a good idea to ride into Parral tonight and let both Gregg and

Hatfield know they intended to hire out to the injured man. Hatfield should also be told that during his absence last night someone had almost demolished his house from the inside.

They made a meal for which neither of them felt much need, washed the dog again, got more water down him, worried in absolute silence because he would not eat, and finally put a plate of food where he could reach it, and went down to the barn to saddle up.

Charley Rivers kept coming back to the question he had asked before. What kind of a man beat a dog with his fists, then tried to kick it to death?

Hank had no answer. There was no need to answer; they both knew what kind of a man that would have to be.

Parral was picturesque and peaceful in the dying day. The roadway was almost empty. There were horses at the tie-rack out front of the saloon, and over in Mex-town someone was playing a guitar, which was a welcome sound as Trainer and Rivers walked their horses down as far as the liverybarn and left them with a raffish-looking Mexican who was the nightman. He told them their friend Walter Ridgeway did not work after five o'clock.

They visited the general store for tobacco and some tinned goods, left the sack out on Doctor Gregg's porch when they went inside, and after telling the doctor what they had encountered at the Hatfield place, asked if he thought his patient in the back room was up to hearing that kind of bad news.

The doctor pondered, and in the end decided that his patient should not be told, then took Rivers and Trainer out into his kitchen, poured each of them a jolt-glass full of amber whiskey and said, "He took a hell of a shellacking night before last. My guess is that he won't even be able to ride out there for another ten days or two weeks."

Charley was gazing at the medical practitioner as though he had not heard correctly. "Doctor, I thought Hatfield got shot."

Gregg nodded. "He did. Shot through the side. Today I talked to some of the men who were in there when it happened. Hatfield was starting to turn away from Cartwright when Cartwright shot him."

Charley was still wearing that troubled expression. "Just now you said he got shellacked."

Joe Gregg's eyes dropped to the whiskey-glass in his big hand. "He did. After he went down Frank Cartwright worked him over."

Charley did not finish his drink. He put the glass aside. "After Hatfield was shot this feller went over and hit and kicked him?"

"Yes. That's what they told me today."

Charley turned to face Hank. Neither of them said anything.

Joe Gregg had a little more to add. "I know how you feel. I felt the same way last night when they brought Hatfield in here. What kind of a town stands by and watches something like that happen?"

Hank nodded at Doctor Gregg. "Yeah, that'll do for openers. What kind of a town *does* stand by and watch something like that?"

Joe Gregg looked from beneath lowered brows. "A town that is in mortal fear of a man who hires his riders because they are willing to hurt people."

Hank was building a smoke when he said, "How many men are in this town, Doctor?"

Gregg colored and scowled. "What difference would that make; these are merchants, not gunfighters."

Hank lit up and blew smoke at the doctor. "Sure they are; merchants. Tell me something, Doctor. You told us there was a cow outfit that adjoined Hatfield; by any chance is that the Balinger outfit, and is the Balinger outfit the one all you big strong fellers are afraid of?"

Joe Gregg straightened up slowly. Hank and Charley had seen that look in his eyes before. "If John Balinger decides he doesn't want you two living on the Hatfield place, you'll find out whether it pays to be careful around him or not."

"Oh hell," said Hank, "we're goin' to be careful, Doctor. That's our business, being careful.

41

Bein' yellow though—that's somethin' different."

Charley led the way back through the house to the front parlor, and with his hand on the latch he eyed Joe Gregg. "Last night we needed an answer from you. Today we still need it. Where is Peter Harkness?"

This time they got an answer which stopped them both in their tracks. "I told you last night, that up until last year no one in this town would have answered that question. And also last night I asked what business it was of yours and who you were."

Charley was leaning on the door with the latch in his grip. "Doc, just answer the damned question, please. Where is Pete Harkness?"

"In the morning when you roll out," Gregg replied, "saddle up and ride almost due north from the Hatfield buildings until you see three tall redstone spires. The In'ians used to hold their religious doings up there. Look for a grave. It's at the base of one of those redstone-men, as the In'ians called them."

Hank quietly said, "That is Peter Harkness?"

"Yes."

"When did he die?"

"I'm not quite sure. More than a year ago, as nearly as I could figure out."

Hank said, "Hell. Doctor, this country is full of graves folks put names to."

Gregg did not dispute this, but he startled them

again. "That man you saw in my back bedroom is the one who buried him."

"Jim Hatfield?"

"Yes. He was the grandson of Pete Harkness. He can tell you all about that burial, and how Pete died. I can only tell you that I treated Pete for bad fainting spells for several years."

Charley was still holding the doorlatch. "Doctor, did you know Pete Harkness was an outlaw with a price on his head?"

Instead of replying Joe Gregg looked long at Charley Rivers. Then he said, "Now I know who you men are—scalp hunters!"

Hank said, "Guess again, and now I guess we're goin' to have to talk to Hatfield after all. Lead the way, Doctor."

Joe Gregg's head went down a little, his shoulder came up in a curving arch as though to protect his chin, and Hank drew his six-gun without haste and cocked it, aimed it squarely at the medical practitioner's brisket and smiled. He did not say a word.

Doctor Gregg looked from the cocked six-gun to the face of the man holding it, then watched Charley release the doorlatch. He heaved mighty shoulders in a shrug which could have signified anything, and turned to head for that small room with the large bed in it, and when he was outside the closed door he faced around to say, "Hatfield is my patient. That's all. If I had a yellow dog in that bed I'd do the best I could for him. Do you understand?"

Hank wigwagged with the six-gun. "Open the door."

Jim Hatfield was sleeping. He did not awaken until Hank leaned and gently brushed his face with a glove. Hank was holstering his six-gun when Hatfield's eyes opened. For moments he simply stared at Trainer and Rivers, then he put an enquiring glance over at Joe Gregg upon the opposite side of the bed. He was mute. So was Doctor Gregg.

Hank said, "Mister Hatfield, we're goin' to dig up your grandpaw."

Hatfield's entire body stiffened as his head came around. The look in his eyes was sharp and quizzical. He stared at both the men standing beside him, and finally as he addressed Hank Trainer he was not the feeble-appearing man he had been.

"If you go near that grave I'll have you shot!"

Hank thumbed back his hat and returned stares with the man in the bed. "You'll do good just to get out of this bed, Mister Hatfield. You're not goin' to have anyone shot." Hank fished inside a shirt pocket and held out his right hand, palm up. There was a small nickel circlet upon it with a star inside the circlet, and in lettering around the edge of the badge was the legend 'Deputy United States Marshal'.

Hatfield stared, but Joe Gregg, across the bed, scarcely more than glanced at the outstretched hand. He had already made his judgment, and it was very close to what had just been substantiated. These rough-looking strangers were lawmen.

Hank put the badge back in his shirt pocket and gestured with a thumb toward Charley Rivers. "Him too. Mister Hatfield, do you have any idea why federal peace officers would want to dig up your grandpaw?"

Hatfield did not make a sound. His eyes never left the faces of the men on the right side of his bed.

"He was an outlaw," explained Charley Rivers. "You knew that. This whole damned town knew it. Well, we didn't expect to find him dead, but if that is really Peter Harkness up yonder in a grave, my partner and I are goin' to be very pleased. We won't make you any trouble. We have three pictures of the old man. We just have to make certain, that's all."

Joe Gregg was frowning. "He's been in his grave over a year. He's not going to look much like any picture you have of him."

Charley did not dispute that. "Most likely you're right, Doctor, but there are other ways of telling and we have enough information about Peter Harkness to make about as good a determination as we'll need. Do *you* know why the federal government is interested in him, Doctor?"

"It was no secret in the Parral country that in his youth Pete Harkness had been an outlaw, had robbed banks and stages and whatnot. I can tell you from knowing him for a long time, whatever he had done as a young man was far behind him. There was no more generous, helpful and considerate human being in this country than Peter Harkness."

Hank was regarding Doctor Gregg when he said, "All right; if he was the local hero, that's fine with us. All we have to verify is that he is dead. That's all. When we've verified that we'll be happy to saddle up and ride out of your town. Anything wrong with that gents? Just one look, then we leave."

Jim Hatfield's face was full of color. He was breathing hard. "If you open my grandfather's grave, neither of you will leave Parral. We'll bury you here!"

Joe Gregg was looking at his disturbed patient when he gestured for the pair of lawmen to precede him out of the room. They obeyed because they had nothing to gain by remaining. When they were out in the corridor and Doctor Gregg had closed the door, Charley said, "Doctor, what in the hell is he all upset about; all we need is verification then he can have his grandpaw in the grave and we'll simply report that Pete Harkness is dead. In these circumstances that is what is

46

required of anyone like us who is serving the law."

Gregg went through to the waiting-room with them before answering. "We've known for years that someday someone would ride into town looking for Pete. Over the years we've talked about it. We decided no one should bother the old man—then he died."

Hank said, "I see. And now that he's dead you're still going to try and prevent anyone from bothering him. Doctor, we're not goin' to bother him. You can come along and help us make the identification."

"I don't think so," said Joe Gregg. "Don't be foolish, just take everyone's word in Parral he's buried out there. What more do you need? Believe me, he is dead."

Charley opened the door, nodded to Joe Gregg and preceded his partner out into the pleasant desert night.

Five

The Redstone Men

They discussed their dilemma from most angles on the ride back out to the Hatfield place. What particularly bothered them was the stubbornness of everyone who knew two lawmen wanted to exhume Pete Harkness. It was not as though they had any designs on the carcass. They were not going to desecrate it. In fact, they were not even going to remove it from the pine box. They just wanted to look in and verify that it was indeed Harkness in his grave.

They reached the yard and were aiming for the front barn opening when Hank said, "You don't reckon those idiots went and buried something with Harkness?"

Charley was dismounting at the barn rack when he said, "Buried what?"

Hank tugged loose his latigo and turned to lead the horse inside when he said, "I don't know. Maybe they didn't bury anything with him, but will you tell me why in hell everyone gets so fired up when we mention lookin' in to make certain it's Harkness?"

They were inside the barn, where it was lightless and still hot when Charley commented, "Maybe that's not Harkness out there, Hank.

Maybe it's an empty coffin. I'll tell you one thing; when we left town they were darned resentful. If we put off goin' up to find that grave, and openin' it, they just might have some lads come out from town to do a little bush-whacking."

They watered the horses out back, stalled them, and trooped to the house for something to eat—and completely forgot about the dog until they opened the door, and he weakly growled at them.

It was an enormous relief. They fired up the kitchen lamp, saw that he had eaten the food they had left and had lapped water, and sank down beside his pallet to talk happily to him. He did not move much, just his head and neck, and once or twice his tail, but he rested his chin on Hank's hand. A man did not require any other acknowl-edgment of gratitude and friendship than that.

An hour later they returned to the barn to seek shovels and a crow-bar, and to rig out again, but this time they rode northward, as Joe Gregg had directed them to do.

There was not much light. In fact visibility was limited to about fifty or sixty yards, but neither Charley nor Hank were particularly worried. Doctor Gregg had said there were three redstone spires, and even on a ghostly night of weak sun-shine something like rock spires would show up.

But they were farther north than the lawmen thought. In fact, they did not see any rocks at all,

49

just some piñons, some lacy little paloverdes, and an occasional barrel cactus until they had been in the saddle almost two hours, by which time they noticed that the landform was changing, and when they came upon a barbed-wire fence with a gate lying on the ground that was also a surprise.

There was grass out there, and even some distant, scattered trees, and finally they saw the spires a mile or so ahead, tall, oddly man-shaped but thin with sloping shoulder-lines which blended into the lower body shapes. There were three of them, each about forty feet tall and standing perhaps ten feet apart. They were unusual; in fact, they were eerie and a little disturbing. There were no other rock spires around. It was easy to imagine Indians being greatly impressed, and incorporating the redstone "people" into their faith and rituals.

They stirred cattle from their beds when they rode down a gradual slope to a wide arroyo with trees and a flowing creek at its bottom. The cattle ran out the opposite creek-willows, and as Charley wrinkled his nose over the familiar scent he drew rein and said, "Remember them tellin' us Hatfield had a fenced parcel called the 'wet section'? I'll make you a bet we're standin' on it."

He was probably correct; Hank was more interested in those redstone plinths, and halted only long enough for his horse to tank up at the muddied creek, then followed the course of the departed cattle until he found a trail heading toward the distant redstone spires.

Obviously, someone had gone to great pains a long time before to clear away all growth around those "redstone people" and to also haul soil and stone in baskets to fill each small depression until the land for an acre or so on all sides was perfectly level.

When Hank dismounted back a short distance and stood at the head of his horse gazing at the three plinths, he told Charley that when he had been a small child back in Ohio his parents had once taken him to a burial at the local cemetery, and he had for the first time encountered a stone Jesus plus a chorus of stone angels, and he had felt then about as he felt now.

Charley was worrying a ragged corner off his plug when he sympathetically nodded his head. At any time the uniquely shaped tall spires would have inspired at least a little awe, but under the circumstances which had brought the partners out here, it went a little deeper and seemed slightly more unnerving.

They did not see the grave. At least there was no rock propped up, nor a wooden cross, but near the base of the northernmost "redstone person" was a barely discernible mound which was unmistakably the length, width, and general shape of a human grave.

Charley Rivers leaned on the crow-bar eyeing the plinths and masticating. Eventually he expectorated, then said, "Hank,—I got this odd feeling. It's got nothin' to do with those man-like big rocks. It's just that I wish I knew a little more'n I do about that grave no one wants us to dig in. Suppose someone taken a few sticks of dynamite, and a few blastin' caps and buried them with old Pete? Dynamite gets awful unstable after it's begun to deteriorate in the ground. Now then— suppose I ram this crow-bar into the grave to loosen the soil so's you can dig."

Hank shook his head without taking his eyes off the northernmost redstone pillar. "That's not it, Charley," he stated, without saying why he was sure of this. "It's what we'll encounter when we prise the top off the coffin."

They went up there to the gravesite and studied it. No particular effort had been made to obliterate vestiges of a grave, which people might normally have done if they'd anticipated difficulty about it.

The ground had settled. Perhaps in another few years it would have settled completely then the outline would have been noticeable as a sunken condition, instead, as now, it was discernible because it was several inches higher than the surrounding area.

Hank turned slowly to scan the countryside in all directions. Visibility was not very extensive, but where he could see there was no indication of other people. Nor did they hear anything, and they stood listening for a while, half prepared to accept a sound of riders approaching.

Charley squinted a long time at the dimensions of the grave, decided which would be the head, and stepped up with his crow-bar. Towering above was the redstone human shape, and Charley spat on his palms, gripped the bar, then glanced up. The recognizable but indistinct face of the pillar was facing eastward, not downward. The redstone man was absolutely impervious to the presence of a pair of grave-violators at his feet.

Charley went to work loosening the soil with his crow-bar so that Hank could shovel it out of the grave and pile it alongside.

There was a particular advantage to digging on the desert when there was no sunlight; men could work steadily and not be driven into the shade every hour or so for water and rest.

There was another advantage, but neither of the federal lawmen knew about it until one of Charley's plunging blows with the steel bar sent back a strong sound of steel striking a hard and unyielding object. Charley thought it was steel, perhaps some part of the coffin, but Hank, with blisters on his hands already, simply said, "Keep breakin' up the ground." The advantage was that this was a shallow grave.

Charley shifted position and began loosening the soil on both sides of the grave until he was down a couple of feet, then he moved to the north and south areas, the head and feet of the coffin.

Hank paused to mop off sweat and catch his second wind while dripping sweat and eyeing his partner's tiring labors. "Suppose," he said, "it's not Harkness down there?"

"It better be," muttered Charley Rivers, who had never been keen on this sort of thing.

"Yeah. But suppose it isn't?" Charley slackened off and leaned on his steel bar eyeing Hank. "I don't know. If it isn't Harkness, then we been lied to—only I don't have that pill roller back in Parral figured to be the kind of a person who lies very much—and otherwise, why would he send us out here, in the first place, if he knew it wasn't Harkness down there?"

Hank went back to turning earth with his shovel as he said, "I don't know. I'm just wondering, is all."

They continued to dig until Hank's shovel would go no deeper, and he slanted it and began clearing soil off the hard metal surface they had struck earlier. It was crowded so Charley climbed out to watch his partner scoop soil off the coffin's top until the entire slightly curved surface was exposed. It was not metal, but it was an extremely hard variety of wood, and where the surface had been scratched, the underlying wood showed a dark, very tight-grained, smoke-shaded red kind of hard wood.

Hank retrieved a broken piece and tossed it up to Charley, who examined the sliver very closely then said, "Whatever it is, Hank, someone had to pay good money to get a coffin made of it imported into this country. It sure as hell isn't any kind of wood I'm familiar with—but for heft and close-grain and all it sure looks like man-zanita."

That drew Hank's attention upward. "Manzanita! You never saw a coffin made of that stuff in your life, and damned little furniture. Manzanita's crooked as a dog's hind leg. You can't make boards out of it."

"All right. What would you say that box is made of?"

Instead of continuing this conversation, which he patently thought had no future, Hank mopped sweat, pitched his shovel up to the ground above, and told Charley to hand down the crow-bar because he was ready to prise up the lid of the coffin.

The lid did not yield. Charley was down on one knee along the crumbly edge of the grave-hole and Hank shifted the tip of the bar to find a good place to obtain a decent purchase for prising.

There were none; the coffin lid fit with sur-prising precision directly onto the sides of the box. Hank raised a face mirroring exasperation and impatience. "No cowtown wood cobbler put this thing together," he exclaimed, and knelt atop the box to run a hand along the edge of the coffin to find just one place where he could insert the sharpened edge of the crow-bar.

Charley had nothing to suggest. He knelt up there watching and scowling, as impatient as his partner. When Hank leaned the bar aside Charley offered a suggestion. "Shoot a hole in one of the corners, Hank; make a hole big enough to get the tip of the bar into, then we'll both lean on the bar."

Hank ignored that suggestion. He had his back to his partner and was down on both knees, now, reaching far under the upper side of the coffin. With a grunt he straightened around, reached for the bar, and very carefully inserted it where he had had his exploring hand.

Charley sensed something and said, "Want me to climb down and help you lean on the bar?"

Hank was gradually increasing his leverage as he said, "Not enough room down here. You stay up there and sort of keep watch."

Charley Rivers looked around and grunted. "Watch for what? Even if they knew we went out to the ranch, or maybe over to the Balinger place, that wouldn't prove nothing."

"Yeah. Well, Charley, not everyone wants to prove things. Maybe they just want to eliminate nosey federal deputies from digging, in which case they could be out yonder drawin' a bead on you right now."

Charley straightened up to make a scowling scan in all directions while his partner got the tip of his bar fitted into the slightly indented place, and eased up to his feet without relinquishing pressure on his crow-bar. He looked up, saw Charley making his scowling search, then Hank began to gently apply pressure on the bar.

He had all his weight on the bar and was about to yield and invite Charley down also to lean on it, when he felt wood yielding under his feet. He gave it one final, powerful wrench, and this time the yielding underfoot was more noticeable. He got over to the weakened edge of the box, reinserted his bar, but deeper this time, then stepped back and lunged downward across the bar. Wood tore, earth crumbled, and the top of the coffin came part way upwards.

Now, Charley offered a hand by going to the opposite side, placing his shovel against the inside of the raised lid, and when Hank nodded, they both exerted pressure and the lid tore loose all around the edges of the coffin. As it came up, Hank had to scramble to avoid being hit by it; there was no space in the hole for maneuvering by anything as large as a man.

He climbed out, got belly-down, strained to reach the upright lid, and with Charley still exerting pressure from the opposite side, they got the coffin lid torn completely loose. But it was surprisingly heavy. Hank had to hold it upright until Charley could come around beside him to also grab the lid, and between the two of them they pulled it up out of the hole and pitched aside, atop the crumbly mound of scabrous soil Hank had been pitching out for more than an hour.

Six

Some Answers

The face with its sightless gaze fixed upon the overhead sky belonged to Peter Harkness. Rivers and Trainer had studied the likeness of Harkness on their way to the lower desert, and whatever the reason, but perhaps as a result of prolonged hot and dry periods in the Parral countryside, the corpse did not appear to have been in his grave more than a few days, maybe a month at the most, and was easily recognizable.

The lawmen were in no hurry. Once they had verified who was in the grave, their earlier wonderment moved them to do a little more exploring. But Harkness's corpse was all the coffin contained. Charley suggested raising the box, looking beneath it, but Hank was recalling how heavy just the lid had been when he shook his head and said, "Let's cover it and get back to the Hatfield place."

They worked in relays because they only had one shovel. Putting the earth back was a little less strenuous than pitching it out, but it still required a fair amount of time. By the time they were finished, were ready to mount up and ride away, the moon was down, the stars had a rusty shading and Hank freed the old jacket from behind his cantle and buttoned it to the gullet.

He looked at Charley as they started back the way they had come and said, "Now, what in the hell was so terrible about that?"

Charley's resonse was dry. "Nothing, unless you count in all the digging."

Hank yawned, reset his hat, watched the bobbing ears of his horse until they were back down near that creek on the wet section, then he twisted to look at Charley who was a yard or so to the rear, and made an observation.

"We did what we came here to do; we didn't have to jump the old devil and take him out of here in irons. Why should the local folks be against us making an identification?"

Rivers was concerned with only his partner's first couple of dozen words. By now he was not just tired and sleepy, he was also hungry, and what they had done this night was completed and he did not really care much about it, not now, not when they had both been able to identify Peter Harkness. "Forget it," he advised, and stood in his stirrups to try and make out rooftops. "We'll be out of their damned country before they know it. I think I can see the buildings. You hungry?"

Hank rolled a smoke. Yes, he was hungry, and he was drowsy. And what no longer bothered his partner at all, still bothered him. Why had everyone been so adverse when he had mentioned finding the Harkness grave and opening it?

"Maybe it's just that they don't want strangers nosing around. I've yet to ride into a town and not have maybe half the population look me over like I was somethin' their dog brought home."

Charley spat, considered the countryside as they approached the Hatfield place, and without much interest said, "When do you want to head out of this country? I'd favor tomorrow."

Hank said, "What do we do about the dog, Charley?" and that stopped Rivers in mid-thought. He had not considered the dog. They were nearing the yard of the Hatfield place in darkness which was becoming chilly, when Charley answered.

"Find someone in town who'll take care of him. Maybe Doc Gregg will let him stay with Hatfield."

Hank abruptly hauled back, sat perfectly still, and raised a hand of warning toward his partner. He had heard walking horses, and while they could be loose animals, he did not think so; loose horses changed direction often. A horse being ridden did not.

They turned southwestward and did not hasten. As they rode they sat twisted to look back. They also prayed that the riders *they* had heard had not heard *them*.

Hank remembered Jim Hatfield's threat—he

would have them shot if they opened his grand-father's grave.

It was probably just talk. Hatfield had been upset.

Quite possibly it was not an enemy at all. As they came to a bosque of trees and worked their way through it, then halted out back, Charley said, "No one likes federal lawmen, and we was warned to stay away from that grave. Whoever is out there—if they're lookin' for us—isn't goin' to be friendly."

Hank held up a gloved hand for silence. They waited a long while but did not hear anything. Hank wagged his head. "I don't think they knew we were out there," he told his partner. "I think they were headin' for the buildings, not the up-country where we came from."

Charley accepted that without comment while he sat his saddle gazing in the direction of the last sounds they had heard. After a while he said, "Let's head for Parral, bed down at the rooming-house, and in the morning have a talk with the pill pusher."

That was what they did, except that by the time they skirted out and around so as not to make any sounds, and eventually got down to Parral, it *was* morning; not sunbright morning, but dawnlight morning. Nor did they bother the proprietor of the rooming-house when they got their old rooms back. So far, they had only met one wide-awake individual: the nightman at the liverybarn.

They slept like logs, did not awaken until nearly noon, and by the time they got down to the café after shaving and otherwise making themselves presentable, it was past midday.

Their old antagonist the caféman showed a wooden expression, got their food and did not open his mouth, not even once.

There was no one in the café. The local feeding-time for the midday meal had come and gone. After eating they sauntered up to Joe Gregg's combination residence and clinic, got a startled look when the medical man opened his front door to their knocking, and after he had closed the door and faced them, he said, "Were you at the Hatfield place last night?"

They had been, but very briefly. Hank answered in a guarded way. "Sort of. Why, was someone lookin' for us?"

Joe Gregg jerked his head. "I have hot coffee in the kitchen." Out there, stoking the woodstove with his back to Rivers and Trainer, he also said, "What about the grave?"

Charley was whittling off a cud when he replied. "You ask a lot of questions, Doc, and the boot's supposed to be on the other foot. We're the ones to ask questions. To start with, who knew we might be at the Hatfield place last night, and who told someone we were goin' to open that grave?"

Joe Gregg rinsed three cups in a bucket of

heating water on his cook-stove as he said, "I can only tell you that Jim Hatfield had a few visitors last night. Beyond that, I have no idea how anyone would know you would be out there. I certainly did not tell anyone."

Charley got the cud fitted exactly where he wanted it before asking another question. "Doc, there is somethin' you can tell us. Why did Hatfield get all roiled up yesterday when we said we were fixin' to open Peter Harkness's grave?"

Gregg put three steaming cups of black coffee on the kitchen table and gestured for his guests to take two of them. As he reached for the third cup he did not do as Hank Trainer expected, he did not pretend he had no idea what Charley had meant. Instead, Joe Gregg took his cup back alongside the drainboard, put a direct, rock-steady gaze upon Charley, and answered bluntly.

"The best thing you boys could have done last night was use the darkness to get a long ways off in. I'm afraid you can't make it now."

Hank and Charley watched Doctor Gregg sip his coffee, then put the cup aside as he started speaking again.

"I am just about impersonal in this," he told the federal deputy marshals. "I did not want you disturbing the grave, but beyond that—and my liking for old Harkness—what is happening now is something else."

Very quietly Hank Trainer said, "What is happening now?"

Joe Gregg lowered his head the way he ordinarily did when he sensed trouble. He balefully regarded his guests. "John Balinger has taken an interest in you."

"Balinger? The big cowman whose rangeboss tried to kill Jim Hatfield?"

"Yes."

Hank said, "How do you know he's interested in us, Doctor?"

"Because last night Glen Butler came over from his café after closing time, and told me he had heard Balinger's rangeboss mention to several of the other Balinger men they would scout up the Hatfield place on their way home, and maybe find a couple of troublesome strangers camped out there."

Charley said, "Doctor, that caféman isn't exactly a feller I'd put a lot of faith in."

Gregg faintly nodded. "I know. He told me about you two. But there is something you don't know. His brother was our town marshal until a month or so ago. He was shot to death while riding north from visiting Jim Hatfield, to the area of the redstone rocks."

Hank and Charley held their coffee-cups and gazed at the medical practitioner for a long time before one of them said, "The impression I get, Doctor, is that someone—maybe this Balinger feller, or maybe Jim Hatfield—is dead serious about not having anyone get interested in the Harkness grave. All right; now tell us why that is?"

Joe Gregg frowned. "I didn't say the town marshal was bushwhacked because of the gravesite. I said he was riding up in that direction when someone shot him off his horse and killed him."

Hank drained his cup and leaned to put it aside. "The caféman, Doctor, what does *he* think?"

Joe Gregg went to stoke the stove again before answering. "He has never liked the Balinger outfit, not Jim Hatfield. He's not a feller who makes a lot of friends."

Hank could have agreed with that, instead he said, "Doctor, what I asked was—what does he think about the killing of his brother?"

Doctor Gregg faced around, head lowered, massive shoulders slumping. "That Frank Cartwright did it."

"Did he?"

Gregg wagged his head. "No. I'd bet my life on it. Frank is disagreeable some of the time, but he's not a murderer. Whoever shot Glen's brother off his horse was lying in some brush and deliberately shot him at close range. That takes a murderer, gents."

Charley broke in to scowlingly take the conversation back to something which he was especially troubled about. "Doctor, what I want to

66

know is, *why* no one wanted that grave opened, and don't tell us because everyone thought Pete Harkness was such a wonderful feller."

Joe Gregg returned to his position alongside the wooden drainboard, leaned there, crossed huge arms across his big chest and stood a while considering his visitors. "You fellers opened the grave, did you?"

Hank nodded. "Yes. Last night."

"And identified Peter Harkness?"

"Yes. We both identified him. He looked pretty fresh and all; maybe it's the dry desert air."

"What else was in the coffin?"

"Nothing," stated Hank. "Not a damned thing. Just the body and the swaddlings."

Joe Gregg continued to stand there, arms crossed, gazing at the pair of federal deputy marshals. Finally, he let his arms drop and went after a refill of his coffee-cup, and while he was pouring he said, "You asked if I knew why the government was interested in old Pete."

"And you didn't answer," murmured Hank Trainer, watching the doctor fill his cup.

"That is true, I didn't answer." Gregg faced around holding his cup. "But I knew, and I suspect that everyone in the Parral countryside knows. John Balinger in particular has pretty well taken over old Pete's secret. Balinger is a person you do not want to cross. He's ruled this part of the south desert for forty years. I've heard enough tales about how he keeps control to have a very wholesome respect for Balinger methods. I never ask any questions, gents, but I hear things, and I can tell you that I do not believe that Balinger has ever found it."

Hank stared steadily at the medical man. "Found what?"

Gregg returned the stare without wavering. "You know exactly what I'm talking about. Old Pete Harkness's cache of diamonds, rubies, and bar-gold. That's what the government has finally tracked him down for, isn't it; that fortune in diamonds, rubies and gold he melted into bars that he robbed from the Butterfield stage which was transporting the Gould-Rockefeller collection from Denver to New York?"

Hank went to work manufacturing a smoke and said nothing. Charley stepped to the rear door to jettison his cud and to afterwards very carefully bar the door from the inside of the room before stepping back over beside his partner to face Doctor Gregg, without saying a word.

Hank lit up and fixed Joe Gregg with his dark gaze. "Everyone knows about this cache, do they, Doctor?"

"Well—I know, and I'm usually the last person around Parral to hear rumors. I would guess that certainly two-thirds of the people in the Parral countryside know. For a fact, John Balinger knows."

"And Hatfield the old man's grandson?"

"Yes, of course. He believed the cache was hidden in the coffin."

"Then why in hell didn't he just dig up the box and look in?"

"Because Balinger has kept an armed man up there day and night since they buried Pete a year or so ago."

Charley squinted. "Who shot the town constable?"

Joe Gregg let go with an unsteady, long breath before saying, "You asked me who Glen Butler believes shot his brother—that is your answer. He thinks Balinger's grave-guard did it."

Hank threw up his hands. "Doctor, no one came anywhere near when we opened that grave. No one took a shot at us. Are you sure you're not just talkin' through your hat about there bein' someone up there to keep folks from opening that grave?"

Joe Gregg bored a look into Hank Trainer. "That grave has been up there more than a year. Most of the people in the countryside know what is supposed to be hidden up there—in the box with Pete Harkness. You saw the grave; had anyone dug in it before?"

Charley and Hank would have had to have answered negatively if they had answered at all. Instead of replying Hank fixed Joe Gregg with his skeptical look and asked a question. "Is that what Hatfield meant yesterday when he said we'd be shot if we tried to open the grave?"

Gregg shrugged. "Probably. I didn't go back into his room after you fellers left until about suppertime. We did not speak. Not a single word."

Hank straightened up. "Doctor, how much of what we've discussed in here this morning do you figure ought to be confidential?"

Joe Gregg did not hesitate at all. "Every bit of it. All that's been said—and one more thing: Balinger had to have a reason for allowing you to open that grave last night. But listen to me, you said all you wanted to do was identify the corpse. Now you have done it. Leave the country. Don't wait an extra hour. Leave. Get out—if you can. Run for it and don't even look back!"

Seven
Trouble

They ate again at the Parral café, and this time their interest in the caféman had nothing to do with the way he cooked, or served, his food. But they made no attempt to engage him in conversation. Which was probably just as well since he was one of those individuals who might inaugurate a conversation, but who resented it when others did.

They got their animals from the liveryman, missed seeing good-natured Walt Ridgeway, and left town with the sun on its downward curve.

Charley was having trouble accepting the possibility that someone had been out there last night when they had opened the grave. He wondered aloud why the grave-guard had not jumped them, and all Hank could come up with was a suggestion that the guard simply had not been up there. For whatever reason—a ride to town for a bottle of whiskey, or the possibility that he was a very hard sleeper, or possibly that he *had* watched them, and for some reason of his own had done nothing. It only occurred to Charley when they had the Hatfield buildings in sight that perhaps the guard out there, with all the time in the world, had already plundered the grave. He

71

mentioned the possibility, and Hank wagged his head.

"Have you forgot already how hard-packed that ground was?" Then Hank put a quizzical look upon his partner and mentioned something which had been on his mind. "If Balinger thought Harkness's loot was in that damned coffin, why hasn't he plundered it long before now?"

Charley had no answer. "I wish the old bastard had been alive. It would have been a lot simpler to sweat it out of him where his cache was than it is trying to find it this way—and one more puzzle, Hank. How's it come no one's stretched him between two trees long before this to get the location of the cache out of him? How long's Peter Harkness lived down here?"

Hank was reaching toward a shirt pocket for his tobacco sack and papers when he caught sight of movement dead ahead among the outbuildings in the Hatfield yard. He went right on reaching, and afterwards, when he was licking the finished quirley and watching the distant yard, he softly said, "If we ride in down there, Charley, they're goin' to bust us."

"Who is? What are you—"

"There's someone in the yard, Charley. I saw movement over by the main-house."

"You sure, Hank?"

"Plumb sure."

"Then change course. Head out due west for a few miles."

Hank had been studying the yard, the buildings, the bits of corral which were visible from the yard and its northern environs. This time the movement was less furtive. He said, "Charley, we rode right in among them."

"Where? I don't see anyone. Who is it? How many of 'em are there?"

"Watch over by the corrals west of the barn. Just keep watching."

They only had another hundred or so yards to cover before entering the yard when Charley cursed under his breath and straightened up in the saddle. He had seen someone off to the west.

"You reckon this is old Balinger?" he asked, sounding indignant.

Hank did not respond as he reined down into the dusty, wide yard and bent half around so as to reach the fir logs dowelled into a pair of rough cedar posts which served as the first tie-rack someone would encounter upon entering the ranchyard.

Charley felt differently. "What the hell do you think you're doing? As soon as you're on the ground, they got us. Stay up there!"

But Hank Trainer was already dismounting, and afterwards he stood there loosening latigos so his cinches would no longer bind, when

73

Charley, still astride, hissed downward. "They got the yard covered. I told you to ride west, damn it."

Hank was dead calm. "Get down, Charley. If we'd busted out to the west they'd have blocked us. Get down and don't act worried. They been waitin' out here for a long spell; they might be mad, Charley."

Rivers swung off and looped his reins, then shifted his cud of chewing tobacco and leaned there watching his partner until a lanky rangeman came around the upper end of the main-house walking toward them without smiling or offering to speak.

Another man appeared dead ahead in the door-less big front barn opening, and from farther to the west two mounted men reined into sight and advanced toward the tie-rack.

A large man came out of the house and stood on the porch, big gloved hands hooked in his shellbelt while he watched that lanky man walk up and say, "Drop the guns, gents."

Instead of obeying, or even acting as though he had heard, Hank straightened around, looked the tall man over, and flung his reins carelessly over the pole as he said, "Who are you, friend?"

The tall man eyed Hank thoughtfully before speaking again. "I ride for Balinger. You see that feller on the porch; that there is Frank Cartwright, Mister Balinger's rangeboss. He's going to have a little talk with you fellers. Now shed them guns or you're goin' to get shot. *Now!*"

Hank dropped his Colt. Charley also did, but with a lot less grace, and Charley's pale blue eyes did not leave the tall rangeman's face.

The tall man turned to watch Frank Cartwright leave the porch on his way down to the front of the barn. Those two mounted men came up as far as the corner of the barn, and sat there. Other Balinger riders came closer, but none of them spoke, nor looked anything but hostile as Hank and Charley looked from man to man.

Hank remembered the big rangeboss from the night at the saloon when he had used his gun to cover the departure of his friends. He also remembered what Joe Gregg had told them about how Frank Cartwright put the boots to a man after shooting him.

Cartwright was a large, powerful man with a bear-trap mouth and small, bullying eyes He halted about fifteen feet from the tie-rack and eyed the deputy U.S. marshals. "Saddletramps," he finally said, making his appraisal of the two strangers in front of him. He knew a little about them; as much as he thought it was necessary to know. "Hired out to mind Hatfield's place while he's laid up, and decided to rob a grave while you was out here where you figured no one'd know."

Charley spat and Hank continued to lean on the rack watching. If there was trouble he and Charley were going to get the worst of it. There were six of them in sight, and Cartwright alone was big enough to grapple with a bear. Guns had been invented for situations like this, but their guns were on the ground beyond reach.

Cartwright walked a little closer and looked malevolently at Hank. "Who are you? What's your name?"

"Name is Hank Trainer. His name is Charley Rivers. We just had an idea about comin' down to the south desert—maybe ride on over the line down into Mexico. Got hired on to sort of mind these buildings by Mister Hatfield in town. That's about the size of it."

Cartwright sneered. "No it ain't the size of it, you son of a bitch. You dug into a man's grave last night. The only thing worse than a horsethief, mister, is a grave robber. There's plenty of places where they hang grave robbers."

The large man took another forward step. He was now close enough to Hank for the deputy marshal to straighten up very slowly off the tie-rack, which was between them. Hank knew what to expect. Not only had he been a peace officer for a long time, but he had also seen his share of brawls; he knew how men maneuvered who were planning to start a fight. He also knew that if he had any chance at all, it was going to be limited to one, first strike. After that it was all going to be the large man's battle.

Cartwright turned slightly to consider Charley Rivers, then he growled scornfully and two of his riders moved in on each side of Rivers, which freed Cartwright for what he had in mind. If Charley made a move they were going to slug him senseless from both sides.

Cartwright had selected Hank for a personal victim by whatever devious method he used in situations of this kind, and now as he balled big fists he wolfishly smiled.

"You'd ought to know better than to ride into new country and take sides, cowboy. That's how they fill graveyards, only this time we're just goin' to teach you some manners. You're lucky."

He moved around the tie-rack without haste. "When you're able, get on those damned horses and don't even so much as stop for a drink of water until you're at least a hunnert miles—"

A rangeman striding briskly came up and whispered in the big man's ear. Cartwright's expression changed several times before the cowboy finished whispering, and stepped away. Cartwright stared at Hank and Charley as though incapable of believing something he had just been told. Finally, he gestured. "Empty them shirt pockets!"

They obeyed, the badges appeared, and Cartwright was not the only surprised man in the

Hatfield yard. He turned to look for that man who had told him these two were federal deputy marshals, did not find him so he faced forward and seemed to be pondering. Eventually he made a gesture, and in a voice of disgust gave an order.

"Get on them damned horses, both of you. We'll leave this up to the boss."

Hank caught Charley's eyes as he turned to tighten the cincha before mounting. Hank winked and rolled his eyes to indicate how narrow their escape had been, then he mounted and watched as two Balinger riders went scuttling around behind the main-house, which was where the rangemen had hidden their mounts.

While they waited, the rangeboss gazed up at his prisoners, and for a long while just stood there looking at them, then he finally wagged his head. "I don't believe it," he growled. "I've seen federal marshals before and they sure didn't look as miserable as you two. Where'd you steal them badges?"

Men appeared with saddled horses, and a youthful rider brought over the rangeboss's animal, which was an eleven hundred pound chestnut with a flaxen mane and tail. A truly magnificent animal, probably too large and hefty for some things, but bound to be among the best at corral roping or dragging long yearlings to the marking fire.

Hank was admiring the chestnut horse when the Balinger rangemen got astride and waited for their rangeboss to give a signal. Cartwright gave it by swinging his romal savagely from one side to the other side; the horse had no warning at all. The sound of hard rawhide against his ribs on both sides was loud, and as the handsome big horse sprang ahead in pain and astonishment Cartwright tore at his mouth with a powerful hand, wrist and arm, to control him.

Charley's breath squeezed out, but to Charley's credit he controlled himself as they all began riding eastward out of the yard.

They loped for a mile, then dropped to a walk. Hank and Charley were certain of their destination although they had never been there before, and when the buildings ultimately appeared they were indeed the buildings Charley and Hank had seen from a distance once before. The buildings they had earlier deduced belonged to a very large cow outfit.

That lanky cowboy who had first walked out into plain sight back at the Hatfield yard eased up to ride upon the far side of Charley Rivers as he said, "Frank gave you good advice back yonder; when you've survived and are able to ride again, mount up and don't never even so much as say you was in the Parral country."

Charley gazed at the tall man, chewed a moment, then spat between them. It was a very near-miss. The tall man reddened, drew rein and allowed Charley to ride on ahead.

Eight
Balinger's Rules

They were kept waiting for more than an hour down at the Balinger bunkhouse. Only one Balinger rider remained inside with them. He was that lanky man who had whispered their identity to the rangeboss over in the Hatfield yard.

He made a smoke and slouched against the only door, eyeing the captives without much interest, and when Charley grumbled the tall man was placating. "Just relax, Marshal. Frettin' won't do any good, and the fact that Cartwright didn't splatter you over yonder, but brought you here instead, most likely means you're not comin' out of this too bad off."

Hank exchanged a long look with the tall man before speaking. "What did you whisper to the rangeboss back yonder?"

"That the pair of you was federal lawmen."

"How did you know that?"

"I heard it in town yesterday."

Hank sighed. So much for the secrecy of Parral.

They heard men approaching the bunkhouse long before the door was flung inward, and Frank Cartwright entered a few steps ahead of a leathery, rough-hewn older man. There was no mistaking John Balinger; he wore a gun with an ivory grip, an engraved silver shellbelt-buckle, and a gold ring on his right hand large enough to choke an alligator.

He was perhaps sixty-five, perhaps seventy-five; many years of exposure had marked him so that it was impossible to guess his age correctly. He halted and gazed at Rivers and Trainer. Cartwright gruffly told him which was which, then also reiterated what he surely must have told the old cowman earlier about Trainer and Rivers, and as they listened Hank and Charley were surprised at the foreman's knowledge. He clearly was not one of those individuals who accepted hearsay without verifying it.

When he finished speaking, Cartwright jerked a thumb in Hank's direction, murmured something the partners were unable to hear, then walked out of the bunkhouse, leaving just Balinger and one slouching cowboy inside with Hank and Charley. The slouching rangeman was that same gangly individual who had been inside the bunkhouse earlier, and right now he got busy paring his fingernails with a Barlow knife, and did not raise his head nor act as though he were listening when John Balinger spoke.

"Why did you dig into Harkness's grave?" the cowman demanded in a gruff tone of voice.

Charley told the blunt truth. "Because we had to verify it really was him."

"You're satisfied now?" growled the older man.

Charley answered shortly. "We're satisfied. It's Pete Harkness."

"Then you'll be ready to leave the country," stated John Balinger, and perhaps unconsciously rested his right hand upon an ivory gun-butt.

Hank spoke quickly because he was not sure how Charley would have answered. "We're ready to leave, except it seems other folks don't want us to."

Balinger made a small, deprecatory gesture with his left hand. "You can leave any time you're a mind to, gents. You can have supper here tonight, we'll hay and grain your saddle-stock, and first thing in the morning you can ride back wherever you came from."

Neither Hank nor Charley took their eyes off the older man's craggy, weathered countenance. Balinger smiled at them. It was the smile of an unctuous cat just before eating the canary.

Charley said, "You're Mister Balinger?"

The older man shifted his attention to Rivers as he inclined his head.

"Did you know, Mister Balinger, that last night I don't think your grave-guard was on the job. We opened it right down to the top of the coffin, and opened that too, without anyone showing up to raise cain over what we were doing."

John Balinger gazed at Charley Rivers as he would have gazed at a troublesome child. "You wanted to look, and so you did it. You came here for Peter Harkness and you found him. I know you're federal lawmen. I know most of the things Harkness did as a young man, and I know the authorities have been looking for Pete for a long while."

Charley had a question. "Do you know why they're lookin' for him?"

Hank winced. If he could have communicated privately with his partner he would have insisted that Charley leave things as they were, so that the two of them could ride off. Balinger had told them they could go. Now, Charley was skirting around a sensitive area and if he was not careful he was going to agitate the cowman who was looking at him as he answered Charley's question.

"I have an idea the law wants back any loot Pete might still have. Well, let me tell you gents something—there is nothing left. I'll tell you a little more. I knew Pete Harkness a long time; close to a quarter of a century. When he came here he was on his way over the line to safety down in Messico. Only he was a sick man. In those days I had some In'ians riding for me. We hid Pete and they worked their medicine on him. It took almost a year, that's how near to bein' dead he was. Afterwards—he wanted to settle here. I traded him some land. What he traded me I took to New York close to twenty years ago and sold for all the money I needed to build up my outfit. Gents, that was the loot, and there's none of it left. Hasn't been any of it left for nearly as many years as you boys are old."

John Balinger went to a scarred old table and perched upon a corner of it. He built a smoke, lighted it, and flipped the match into a big square box full of sand in the center of which stood the bunkhouse cuspidor.

"There was nothin' in the grave, gents. I could have told you that."

Hank shoved back his hat and eyed the older man. Balinger was a member of a tribe of people Hank knew very well. His own father and uncles had belonged to it. Hard, unsmiling, absolutely practical, fearless men who had their own codes and rules. They were usually colorless. They were also usually dangerous men to cross, but Hank took the chance because he understood this kind of man. He said, "You let everyone in Parral believe something was hidden in the coffin—why?"

Balinger knocked ash off his quirley before replying. "No. That was his grandson, it wasn't me, Marshal." Balinger's hard, steady eyes rested upon Hank Trainer. "Old Pete and I were close to bein' partners. He was as good a friend as I ever had. His grandson—well, he came out here because Pete sent for him. Pete was ailing and old; he wanted some blood kin around. I had doubts but didn't say anything. He sent for the feller—and he come out—and boys, a son of a bitch like Jim Hatfield makes an outlaw like old Pete Harkness look better'n better."

Charley said, "Why?" and John Balinger switched his attention to Rivers when he replied.

"Because he is a damned parasite. First, he made Pete leave his sick bed and take him over his ranch."

"What for? Couldn't Pete have drawn him a map of the corners?"

Balinger snorted. "Corners hell; he didn't give a damn about the land—he thought his grandfather had caches of gold about the land and whatnot hidden away. Pete died. His grandson passed word around that there was hidden loot on the place—he even said there was somethin' hidden in the old man's grave—wouldn't allow old Pete to lie easy in his ironwood coffin. You boys see that box? I sent to Ohio to have that made; two of 'em, one for old Pete, one for me. Well, anyway, damned if I was going to let folks bother old Pete. I put a man up there and he knocked a few heads together and sort of discouraged folks." Balinger paused and continued to gaze at Charley, except that now his tough eyes showed bleak amusement. "He warn't up there last night, you said? The hell he warn't. He could have blown your gawddamned skull apart any time—but I sent word up to let you two fellers dig. You were lawmen and all you wanted was to see old Pete's face."

Balinger stepped over and dropped his smoke into the cuspidor, then he straightened around. "All right, gents, now you tell me what you're goin' to do when you leave my yard, and dependin' on what that is I'll tell you how far you're goin' to get after you leave. I don't think either one of you is a liar, and I give you my word I ain't one either. You talk straight with me and we'll part company smilin' at each other."

That lanky man over by the door had finished paring all ten of his fingernails, clicked the Barlow knife closed, pocketed it and straightened up looking dispassionately at Rivers and Trainer—and a sudden intuition told Hank who that man was: Balinger's grave-guard sure as hell.

Charley blew out a noisy breath and looked at his partner. Hank saw the look and understood it. Charley wanted a private discussion. The look on John Balinger's face said there was not going to be anything like that; that whatever decisions were reached were going to be reached here and now, spontaneously and without equivocation. Hank, himself, felt pretty much the same way, but there was something which required clearing up, so he said, "Mister Balinger, there was some gold, some diamonds and some rubies."

Balinger did not even bat an eye. "Yeah. And there was a box of Mex chalices, crucifixes, altar candlesticks—solid gold and heavy as hell, all of it, gents, and inset with emeralds and topaz and stones I didn't even know the names of."

Hank softly said. "And—"

"Marshal, it went back to the Mex government. Do you want to know what they gave me in exchange? Total support from the Mex government within the law, in their country, for anything I do as long as I live." Balinger's wide, thin mouth quirked a little at the corners. "I've used that once in a while when Mex rustlers and horsethieves have raided up around Parral."

"None of that stuff went to New York to be sold?" asked Hank, and Balinger slowly shook his head. "None of it. Not so much as one candlestick of it. But I never told Pete that; I let him think I sold it. Pete wasn't much of a believer."

"But you are?"

"No. No more than Pete was, except that I don't believe churches should be robbed, an' that's all I got to say on that subject. The other loot, the things you mentioned, that's what I took to New York and sold. They broke it up and resold it. Gents, you'd never find it, not now after all those years." Balinger went over by the

87

table and crossed both arms over his chest. "What are you goin' to do after you leave here, boys?"

Hank shot Charley a glance, then faced old Balinger, and mirthlessly smiled. "Go back, write out our report about Harkness being dead, verify it, say we found no loot but heard dozens of tales about there having been some, and turn in the report—and wait."

"Wait?"

"Yeah. Wait and see what the U.S. Marshal decides to do."

"What do you expect he'll do?"

"Nothing he hasn't already done. Harkness belonged to another generation, Mister Balinger—so do you—so does that loot no one is ever going to recover. If the Marshal wanted to try and prosecute you for accepting stolen goods, he'd have to rely on your own testimony that you got it from Harkness; there's no one left other than you. Would you testify against yourself?"

Balinger did not reply. He unfolded his arms, looked at the tall cowboy and jerked his head for the man to leave the bunkhouse. When they were alone Balinger said, "Tell you what, boys, I been a fair judge of men all my life. That's why I kept Pete down here and traded him all that land. I like havin' decent neighbors. Now then, I've got twelve thousand acres over northwest of the red-stone country, which if you was to split it down

88

the middle would make six thousand acres for each one of you and—"

Hank laughed out loud. The first time he had done that in months. The sound startled his partner. It also stopped John Balinger in mid-sentence.

Hank checked his laughter and said, "No thanks. If you want to do us a favor, Mister Balinger, quit grazing your cattle on that wet section and quit deliberately trying to push Pete Harkness's grandson into a killin' fight. You don't have to like him; maybe he's as big a fraud as you claim, but you're not every man's judge either."

Balinger rocked up onto his toes and back onto his heels and squinted at Hank for a moment, then turned abruptly toward the door. "Time to eat," he said, and led the way out of the bunkhouse.

Over in front of the big old barn there were half a dozen tough-looking cowboys loitering. Clearly, if there had been any loud shouting or other sounds of disagreement emanating from the bunkhouse, those rangemen would have walked over there and made mincemeat out of a pair of federal lawmen.

One man in particular kept his eyes on Hank and Charley; Balinger's rangeboss, Frank Cartwright.

Nine

Some Questions

They had supper at the Balinger place but did not spend the night there. John Balinger walked down to the corral with them and leaned on the tie-rack watching as they rigged out. He said, "I don't expect you fellers would let me know in advance if trouble was comin' from the U.S. Marshal."

Hank agreed with that. "We wouldn't, any more than we'd tip your hand if you were goin' for someone. But I doubt that you have much to worry about."

Balinger shrugged. "Maybe not. But there's Jim Hatfield. He'll make trouble for me any way that he can. He's tried doing that ever since he arrived down here."

Hank was remembering the appearance of Hatfield when he dryly said, "Looks the other way around, Mister Balinger. Your rangeboss not only baited him into a gunfight, but after he'd shot Hatfield down he went over and put the boots to him. That didn't seem to us like he was bothering you, more like you were botherin' him."

Balinger did not argue, which was one thing the lawmen had noticed about him. He would say whatever it was he had on his mind, and he would listen to whatever someone else said in return, but he would not come back and argue. Now, he watched the lawmen get astride, hauled upright on the rack and said, "Good luck, boys. You goin' down to Parral before heading out?"

They were, they told him, because they had their bedding and whatnot at the rooming-house. They thanked him for his hospitality, nodded and rode off through the soft, warm night.

For a long time neither of them had anything to say. In fact, not until they had the Hatfield rooftops in sight did Charley suggest that they look in on the dog.

This time when they entered the yard there was no one waiting, and the harness horses out back nickered for a handout. They forked feed to them, crossed to the rack out front of the main-house, left their horses drowsing there and went indoors. They did not bother lighting a lamp, just the stub of an old candle.

The dog was pleased to see them. He was out of water and hungry. They took care of those things, talked to him, watched him stand on all fours, none too steadily, and discussed his future. He was not up to being carried across a saddle all the way to Parral, and if they did not take him down there tonight they would have to return for him tomorrow with a buggy.

Charley looked down at the unsteady animal.

"We'll come back with a rig. What the hell; there's no time limit on when we got to get back up north."

They left the dog with plenty of feed and water, got back astride and headed for Parral. Midway along Charley said, "Six thousand acres each would be a fair slice of country, Hank."

"Not down here it wouldn't, Charley. My guess is that you got to figure maybe three hunnert acres per head. Anyway, I never liked the idea of acceptin' land from a man who wants to pick his neighbors so's he can be the head In'ian and all the rest of us'd be the peons. Even if Balinger seems to be a decent sort of man, I still don't want anythin' from him."

Charley sighed. "Well, it looks like lousy cow country anyway."

They reached Parral after the town had locked up and turned in for the night, and did as they had done before, left their horses to be cared for at the liverybarn, and went along to the rooming-house, but this time the proprietor was waiting for them, or at least had not retired yet, and they had to pay up, after which the proprietor departed and the partners went to their rooms.

It had been a long and eventful day. Charley was asleep within moments of rolling in, and Hank stood a moment by his roadway window having a smoke and getting sleepier by the moment. He was more given to reflection than

Charley was; he was willing to accept the judgment he had made of Balinger, but there remained a few troublesome thoughts to keep him by the window for a while yet. One was the way the town marshal had died—out by those redstone pinnacles, shot from ambush—and another thing was Balinger keeping as his range-boss a man who obviously was cruel and vicious.

Finally, he bedded down, put everything out of his mind and slept like a log until sunup and town sounds roused him.

He met Charley out back at the wash-rack, and they grunted at each other. Later, when they met again out front on the porch, fully dressed, shaved and ready for the day, they walked down to the café without a word passing between them, walked in, glanced at the half-dozen or so other diners along the counter, breathed deeply of coffee aroma, and got two places at the counter.

This time the caféman took their orders immediately, and brought coffee before going out back to his stove. Charley sipped, looked around the room, nudged his partner and jerked his head without speaking.

Doctor Gregg was up the counter and evidently had not seen Rivers and Trainer enter. He was reading something, a letter perhaps or a small newspaper, while he ate.

Their food came, the caféman looked at each of them, they nodded at him and he walked away.

The breakfast was excellent. Even if it hadn't been it would still have made a difference. Trainer and Rivers were men for whom this world held no delights until after they'd tanked up first thing on black java. Afterwards they acted reasonably civilized.

Diners came and went. Doctor Gregg paid up and departed still engrossed in whatever it was he had been reading. If he recognized Trainer and Rivers he gave no indication of it. They were not upset; they were hungry, and when the caféman came along to refill their coffee-cups, Hank paused at his feeding to study the unsmiling face opposite him, and say, "Would you mind a personal question this early in the morning?"

The caféman straightened up and regarded Hank stonily. "I mind personal questions any time, Marshal."

Hank watched the man walk briskly back in the direction of his curtained-off cooking area, and blew out a big breath while reaching for the refilled cup. "You hear what he called me, Charley?"

"Marshal."

"Yeah. I know something about this town. If you want to keep a secret, tell it first."

Charley continued eating. He had never thought keeping their official identity a secret was necessary. The caféman abruptly returned and scowled at Hank. "What personal question?" he demanded.

Hank stroked his chin; women were usually like this, unable to control their curiosity, but men were commonly more disinterested—except for a few, like this caféman, who could not stand *not* knowing.

Hank leaned on the countertop with his thick crockery coffee-cup curled into one large hand, and gazed steadily at the caféman. "Since the day your brother, the constable, was bushwhacked up by those redstone figures, have you learned anything about the man who shot him?"

The caféman made an unconscious big swipe of the countertop with a damp cloth from his belt, and avoided meeting the glances of either of the lawmen. He was a long time replying. When he finally did it, he raised sulphurous eyes.

"Nothing. Why would anyone tell me? Do you want to know what I *think* happened? Balinger ordered it done, and someone like Frank Cartwright did it."

"Why?" asked Hank.

"Why? I can think of several reasons. For one thing, old Balinger's like that, and he don't hire any riders who aren't just as mean and ornery. For another thing, maybe my brother discovered somethin' about the Harkness loot. Everyone knows it's out there some place, and maybe my

brother, being in a position to find things out—"
The caféman let it trail off while he gazed
steadily at Hank and Charley. The last thing he
said before hiking back up the counter to look
after one of his diners was more a growl than a
statement.

"Balinger runs the Parral country like he was
king of it. My brother ain't the first man who
came back to town belly down across a saddle.
You keep nosin' around and you'll end up the
same way."

After breakfast Hank and Charley went out into
the newday sunshine and watched Walt
Ridgeway lead a team out of the yard and back it
onto the tongue of a light spring wagon.

Walt was a good hand with livestock. He had
those horses hitched to the trees and yoked to the
tongue in less time than it would have taken most
men.

A couple of strangers sauntered forth from the
barn to climb up to the seat of the spring wagon
and get ready to drive away. Charley lifted his
hat to scratch. Those men looked like miners to
him. If there was any worthwhile mining to be
done on the south desert, it was in the local
graveyards where there were gold teeth. Charley
watched the rig move past, and brushed Hank's
arm. "What the hell will they be up to?"

Hank had not paid much attention to the rig or
the men who had hired it. He had been watching

Walt Ridgeway, and now he struck off in the direction of the big, faggot-fenced yard into which he had seen Walt disappear.

Charley trooped along in silence. Even after they found Walt over beside a big old leaky stone trough putting Bull Durham sacks of asafoetida into the brackish water, Charley was still pondering the mystery of the two strangers with the look of miners to them.

Ridgeway grinned broadly and said, "Hell I thought maybe you boys had left the country."

Hank's reply was partially true. "Just gettin' acquainted with the country, Walt. It's big, and it's empty, and interesting. Were those miners who just drove off in the spring wagon?"

Ridgeway's blue eyes, nearly hidden when he smiled, showed an expression of concern when he answered. "Yeah, I expect you could call 'em miners. Just got to town last night. Hired that rig to go down to the old mission ruins below Mextown and look for relics."

Hank willingly accepted that explanation. He did not care what the strangers were up to, he had simply wanted an opener to get Walt talking.

"You were around when the town constable was ambushed, Walt?"

"Yep, sure was. I was the feller who lifted him down when they brought him into town."

"Who brought him in?"

"A couple of old Messicans who had been out

with their burros gathering faggots for their cookin' fires."

"What did they say, Walt?"

"About what? They found him out near those red-rock spires, he hadn't been dead long, and they hauled him to town. That's about the size of it."

"They didn't see anything, Walt?"

"No. Not that I know of. They just helped me lift him off the horse, lay him out on the ground, then they went off leading their burros, heading for Mex-town." The hostler eyed Hank with his smile fading. "Go hunt them up. They are brothers and their name is Sanchez; reliable fellers. I've known 'em for years."

Hank nodded as though he would take Walt Ridgeway's advice, led the way back to the roadway out of the corralyard, and when Charley halted in overhang shade to gnaw at his cut plug, Hank said, "How is your Spanish?"

Charley spat before replying. "Terrible. Maybe they know English. Mostly, they do when they live close to a *gringo* town. You ready to go over there?"

Hank shook his head and turned southward. Charley shrugged. He had enjoyed a long night of sleep, had gotten around an excellent breakfast, the day was still benignly cool, Charley had a cud of tobacco cured in blackstrap molasses in his cheek, and as far as he was concerned, one place in Parral was as good as another place.

Only when Hank turned in past the picket fence out front of Joe Gregg's place did it occur to Charley where they were going.

The big older man opened the door and led them into his waiting-room with nothing more than a grunt of welcome. He had been wiping his hands on a clean cloth when he had answered the door. Now, turning to face his visitors, he finished with the towel and shoved it under his belt.

Hank smiled. "How's the patient?"

Joe Gregg's gaze was neither friendly nor hostile; it was cool and skeptical. "He's coming right along. I misjudged his physical condition, I'm afraid. Jim will be ready to leave my place in another two or three days. Of course he can't rush home and go out roping cattle, but for lesser chores he'll be fine. You want to talk to him?"

Hank was agreeable to that, so Doctor Gregg did as he had done before, he led the way almost to the closed door of the wounded man, then halted and turned to admonish them against upsetting Hatfield.

Hank smiled and waited until the door had been opened, "I'll do my best, Doctor."

Ten

Cartwright

Jim Hatfield did indeed look much better. In fact he scarcely resembled the ailing man Hank and Charley had spoken to only the day before yesterday. His color was good, his eyes were bright, his attention was unwavering as he considered the pair of federal lawmen.

He knew the pair of saddletramps he had hired to look after his property while he was incapacitated were not drifters; like everyone else in the area who had any interest in Trainer and Rivers, Hatfield knew they were federal deputy marshals, and before they had an opportunity to mention that he looked much improved, Hatfield said, "I want to sign a warrant against John Balinger and his rangeboss."

Hank smiled. "Go right ahead, but without a lawman in Parral you might have some problems."

"You—" exclaimed the man in the bed—"you two can serve them, arrest them both and fetch them to town to be locked up."

Charley shook his head at Hatfield. "You have to use your own lawman. We aren't authorized to do anything like you want done."

Hatfield's color was mounting when Hank

said, "Are you sure your grandfather left a cache?"

Hatfield's eyes swung to Hank. "I'm sure. He told me he left not just one, but several. Balinger's going to kill me, and anyone else, to prevent those caches from being found."

Hank was sympathetic. "He's got an armed guard up at your grandfather's grave. Did you know that?"

"Of course I knew it," exclaimed Hatfield. "Who do you suppose bushwhacked the town constable? And that's not all the guard has done."

"Why?" asked Hank.

That seemed to stop Hatfield in his tracks. "Why? Why? Because one of the caches is out there, that's why, and Balinger knows it."

"If he knows it why doesn't he dig your grandpaw up and get the loot?"

"Because he dasn't. I keep watch up there. I told the town marshal about that gunman hiding out up there. That's where he was going when they ambushed and killed him."

Hank ignored Hatfield's digressions and clung to the central theme of their earlier discussion. "I'll tell you something, Mister Hatfield. There is no buried loot at your grandfather's grave. My partner and I dug down and opened the coffin. There is nothing there but a dead man in a coffin made of red ironwood."

For a long moment Hatfield seemed too

stunned to react, then he said, "You're lying. They'd never let you do that."

Charley fished around among his pockets until he found that sliver of very hard reddish wood Hank had tossed up to him at the gravesite. He held it up toward Hatfield, then pitched it over atop the counterpane.

"That's from your grandpappy's box," he announced, and watched Hatfield lift the sliver and closely examine it. "There is no way to get something like that without digging your grand-pappy up, and that's what we did."

Doctor Gregg's voice was husky when he said, "You opened the grave and found nothing?"

Hank turned slightly in order to be able to see the man in the bed. "Nothing. Just that piece of wood." He swung his attention back to the med-ical man. Joe Gregg's expression was a com-posite of several emotions and Hank could make out none of them. When he faced around again Hatfield was staring intently at him. Eventually, when Charley was about to open the door for their departure, Jim Hatfield said, "Joe, there is your answer," and held up the sliver of red iron-wood. "They found Balinger's man. Most likely they killed him. Maybe they even buried him in the same hole after they dug into the grave and stole the cache. This here piece of wood—like they said—a man couldn't get it unless he dug into the grave and opened it."

Hank and Charley were staring at Jim Hatfield, stunned at how he had twisted the significance of the little piece of wood. The doctor slowly swung his head until he was looking at Rivers and Trainer. He said nothing, just stood looking, and when Charley got it all straightened out in his head he scowled at Joe Gregg.

"You better put leg irons on your patient, he's nutty as a fruitcake. Hank told you the gospel truth—there was nothin' in that coffin but a dead man and the blankets they rolled him up in. Come on, Hank, I need fresh air."

They stamped out onto the porch before Charley halted and looked at Hank Trainer. "Did you get the same feelin' back there I got? Like Joe Gregg an' Jim Hatfield are in some kind of partnership?"

Hank nudged his partner, jutted his jaw, and struck out for the saloon. It was hot outside, the sun was boring down, Parral seemed to have decided it was siesta time because there was no one abroad, not even down in front of the general store, and when they entered the saloon it too was nearly deserted. Three rangemen were slouching at the bar and two old men were playing cards in the northwest corner of the big old room, near a window.

The barman looked forlorn. Every time Hank and Charley had seen him he had looked that way. They got a bottle and two glasses, went down around the lower curve of the bar, for privacy, and settled in for a couple of drinks. No one heeded them, not even the dolorous-faced barman.

Hank said, "Remember what Balinger told us about Hatfield making out like there was a cache full of loot? I think he knew what he was talking about, Charley. Did you see the expression on the doctor's face when we talked about opening that grave and only finding a dead man in it?"

Charley had seen the expression, and he had noticed something else. "Just before we left, that sawbones had me feelin' that what we said contradicted what Hatfield had told him. He looked a little like a man who's about to be sick to his stomach."

Hank downed his whiskey and pushed the glass aside. "Why? Is there really a cache?"

Charley scoffed. "Naw. I'd take Balinger's word any day of the week. But even if I wouldn't, and he lied to us, I can tell you one thing about a man like John Balinger—if he had twenty years to find a cache, believe me, he'd sure as hell have found it. Hank, any way you look at it, there's no cache."

Hank considered the whiskey bottle. In the end he did not refill his glass. "What's botherin' me, is *why* everyone is so dead-set on having folks believe there is a cache—and when you pin them down they'll tell you there isn't one."

The barman came along to measure the amount of whiskey they had poured from the bottle. They paid him according to his finger measurement and waited until he had departed before reverting to their earlier topic, and this time they did not get very far either because several horsemen loped noisily up to the rack out front, unloaded, tied the horses and came clumping inside out of the heat.

The first man through the swinging doors was Balinger's big rangeboss, Frank Cartwright. Behind him came four men Hank and Charley recognized as having been among the ambushers who had caught them at the Hatfield place last night. One man was not present, that gangling, tall man, but there was a younger rider in the tall man's place. He looked to be no more than perhaps seventeen or eighteen years old, and although he was as desert-scorched as the others, and made a good effort to act as important as the older men acted, he did not quite manage it.

Cartwright saw Hank and Charley, gazed briefly at them, then became busy with a whiskey bottle which was moving around up where the Balinger men had come to rest.

Charley considered another drink, and finally yielded. After downing it he softly said, "Hank, you don't reckon old Balinger sent them in to make certain we'd left, do you?"

Trainer had not considered that. He scarcely

considered it now as he answered in the same subdued tone of voice. "Maybe, Charley. With a man like John Balinger you got to be standin' right beside them to know what they figure to do, and by golly, about half the time you guess wrong anyway."

Cartwright finished with the whiskey bottle. He downed his first jolt, rolled his eyes, and at the expressions of amusement among his men he rolled his eyes again, then laughed. He had scarcely finished laughing when he faced the lower end of the bar. "You fellers still around? I thought the old man told you to quit the country."

It was not so much the words as the way they had been spoken which annoyed Hank Trainer as he leaned there gazing up the bar. He did not answer, and neither did Charley. Most of the other men in the saloon did not notice, but Frank Cartwright noticed that he had been ignored. The humor left, he reached for the bottle again, and the dolorous-faced barman, whose business it was to anticipate things, looked anxiously from the rangeboss to the pair of men at the lower end of his bar. He probably would have ordered Hank and Charley to leave his saloon, if he'd been able to do that; now, though, it was too late.

Cartwright downed his second jolt. The bottle left his hand and began its second tour among the other rangeriders; they were more interested in the bottle's progress than in anything else, and were therefore caught by surprise when the rangeboss pushed back from the bar facing southward.

"Federal marshals," exclaimed the rangeboss, scorn in his words. "Regular rip-roarin' U.S. deputy marshals! You know what you fellers look like to me—a pair of lice-carryin' saddletramps who stole a couple of badges somewhere."

Charley straightened up slowly. Hank was gazing at the rangeboss while still leaning on the bartop. The only other man to move was the bartender. His normal expression of despair deepened as he shuffled over near the rangeboss and softly said, "They aren't botherin' anything, Frank. Here, have one on the house."

Those two jolts hit big Frank Cartwright at about the same time. His color deepened and his eyes brightened. Hank, who had made his assessment of Cartwright several days earlier, watched the transformation, and with his right hand out of sight below the bar, tugged loose the tie-down thong which held the six-gun in its holster on his right side.

The rangeriders were no longer jostling each other and pouring whiskey. They were lined along the bar behind their rangeboss, suddenly as still and watchful as men could be.

Only that troubled barman continued to speak in a whining manner to the rangeboss, urging restraint. He might as well have been talking to an adobe wall. Hank and Charley knew the barman had a sawed-off shotgun on a shelf beneath his bar. That kind of a weapon was standard equipment in saloons. They also suspected that the barman would not use it.

Cartwright's menacing stare did not appear to be accomplishing much, so he said, "Mister Balinger told you sons of bitches to get out of Parral. When Mister Balinger tells scums bastards like you fellers to do something, and they don't do it—"

Cartwright stepped a little farther away from the bar. He was in view almost as far down as his knees but the men he was challenging were still more than half hidden by the bar.

Cartwright was not drunk; two jolts could not accomplish that, but they had made him reckless and deadly. The men behind him were like statues. Even the forlorn barman was no longer making an attempt to prevent trouble. He had both hands below the bar, but he was not moving either, when Cartwright spoke again—in a lethal, flat tone of voice this time.

"Step out from behind that bar, you saddle-tramps—one at a time or both at the same time. *Move, you yeller sons of bitches!*"

Charley moved but Hank was still slouching against the bar, motionless, his eyes fixed upon big Frank Cartwright. When Charley cleared the lower end of the bar, both he and Hank saw the faint signal they were watching for. Cartwright's

heavy right shoulder sagged almost impercep-
tibly and Charley swung sideways, drew and
fired, all at the same time. He fired three times,
each gunshot rolling over into the next one.

The barman jerked at his shotgun, and one of
the Balinger cowboys swung a steel Colt-barrel
across the barman's wrist. The barman dropped
his scattergun, screamed and spun away holding
his broken arm with his uninjured arm, ready to
be sick to his stomach.

Hank's weapon was atop the bar and cocked as
the gunfire ended and powder smoke began to
spread. A cowboy yelled defiantly and crouched
to draw. Hank shot the man through the head,
and his hat, with red froth inside it, struck a man
across the face who had been directly to the rear.

It was over.

There were three stunned rangemen at the bar.
That youngest cowboy, the one who had been
trying so hard to emulate the older men, was
dead on the floor from Hank Trainer's slug, and
Frank Cartwright was lying on his face with
blood puddling beneath him, his gun five feet
distant where it had slipped from his fingers. It
was not even cocked. The big bullying Balinger
rangeboss had come to that point in his career
they all came to eventually, when they thought
they were invincible. He had met a man who was
more experienced and much more deadly, but
who did not look as though he would be.

Eleven
Doctor Gregg's Patient

There was no one in sight as they herded the dis-
armed rangemen over to the Parral jailhouse and
locked them in, then draped their guns from
wall-pegs and left the hats of their prisoners,
each hat containing the personal property of a
prisoner, atop the late lawman's dusty old desk
while they returned to the saloon, and discovered
that someone had scuttled for Doctor Gregg, who
was down on one knee beside Frank Cartwright.
There was no point in examining the younger
cowboy; his brains and part of his skull were visible inside his nearby hat. Gregg glanced up at
Trainer and Rivers, said nothing, and resumed
his examination of John Balinger's dead rangeboss.

The barman was around in front of his bar
clutching a soiled bar rag and looking more
dolorous than ever as he said, "It was Frank,
Doctor," and Gregg shoved up to his feet and
made his own remark about that. "It was always
Frank. This time he made a mistake. The Frank
Cartwrights in this world always make a mistake,
sooner or later." Joe Gregg looked at Hank and
Charley without a shred of friendliness showing.
"Which one of you got him?"

Charley frowned. "What business is that of yours? All you got to do is certify that he's dead, and pump him up for burying. I got him. Hank got the other one. If you want to know the rest of it, we got the other Balinger riders locked into cells across the road."

Joe Gregg lowered his head and peered from beneath thick brows at the pair of lawmen. "You better send someone to the ranch so Mister Balinger can come to town with his wagon and haul the bodies out to be buried. There's no point in me embalming them until he gets here and says it should be done."

Gregg looked around. There had not been many customers in the bar before; there were fewer now. He addressed two men who were looking on from up the bar, asking if they would carry the corpses over to his shed across the alley. The men neither moved away from the bar nor spoke, so Doctor Gregg mentioned a fee, and both men left their empty glasses and approached the bodies.

The barman showed Gregg his swelling and discolored arm. Doctor Gregg looked more annoyed than compassionate as he instructed the barman to visit him at his cottage when it was convenient, then started out through the batwing doors with Charley and Hank behind him. They caught him near the roadway hitch-rack and Charley said, "One question, Doctor. A while ago at your house when we talked about opening old Harkness's grave, I got the impression you wasn't too happy—why?"

Joe Gregg pushed big hands into the pockets of a shapeless old coat and considered his interrogator. "You should have saddled up and left Parral," he said, ignoring Charley's question. "Have you any idea what John Balinger does to men who make trouble with his riders?"

Hank said, "Doctor, people don't get in much trouble mindin' their own business. Let us sweat about Balinger; you just answer Charley's question. Why were you upset when we said that coffin up yonder was empty except for the old man in it, and some cloth they'd wrapped him in?"

Joe Gregg continued to stand with both hands in his pockets gazing at the federal marshals. For a long time he did not move his glance or open his mouth, and during that interim the pair of townsmen he had hired to carry the bodies from the saloon to his embalming shed went by with defunct Frank Cartwright. He was all the dead weight two men would care to struggle with, so they would have to return for the other dead man.

Finally, Doctor Gregg said, "Follow me out of this sunshine," and led the way to the opposite plankwalk and northward to an overhang which jutted over the planks out front of the saddle and harness works. He stopped there and mopped perspiration before speaking. "I joined the combine of investors Jim Hatfield formed." As he said this Doctor Gregg did not meet the glance of either of the men standing in shade with him. What those two men had done was make a fool of Joe Gregg, inadvertently, of course, but still a fool. He was having difficulty talking about it, and if the men standing there listening had not been federal lawmen, Gregg probably would not have spoken at all.

"We each paid Jim seven hundred dollars for a share of the caches his grandfather hid around the Hatfield place. One cache was supposed to be in the coffin with the old man. It wasn't. You men opened the grave and found nothing. Jim said you two had no doubt found the loot and had stolen it." Finally the medical practitioner turned to meet the steady stares he was getting. "I did not believe that, and after you left the room I told Jim I didn't believe you two had stolen the cache, because I did not believe there had ever been one up there at the gravesite."

Charley was frowning. He and Hank had been puzzled by all the secrecy surrounding those supposed caches. They had believed it when Balinger said that there was no cache, but with the inherent reservations men would automatically have in those circumstances. What they had just heard from the doctor fitted something John Balinger had hinted at, at his bunkhouse, about

113

how Hatfield had devised a way to capitalize on the infamy of his grandfather; he had not only done that, but he had done it on a large scale. The next step for Hatfield, now that his deception had been unmasked, was to take his wealth and flee.

Hank said, "Who are the other investors. Doctor?"

Gregg mentioned a number of names neither of the federal lawmen had ever heard before, then he waved his arms. "They're scattered over the Territory. I had no idea how many there were until a little while ago. He has been selling shares through the mails too."

Hank sighed. "He told you that?"

"Yes. We were talking—arguing, I was mad as hell—when someone came from the saloon to say I was needed over there. He told me he'd been peddling shares since the month his grand-father died, and that he had enough money put away in an eastern bank to live on for the rest of his life. He said I could have the ranch. Then he laughed as he got dressed."

Charley stared. "Got dressed?"

"Yes. He was well enough. It was an almost miraculous recovery. He won't be able to do much for a while, but he can drive a rig and in a pinch could ride. Just nothing strenuous."

Hank dryly said, "Or ride one of the steam cars that head for the east every day out of Denver and some other big towns." Hank jerked his head

114

and began walking briskly in the direction of the medical man's cottage.

He was not hopeful and neither was Charley. Back down where they had left Joe Gregg, the doctor had not moved. Evidently too much had happened in a short space of time in a community where nothing much ever happened. Joe Gregg was still nonplussed. Two killings in one day, and the discovery that he had been duped too, was more than he was prepared to accept on a moment's notice.

It would not have made any difference if he had returned to his cottage with the lawmen anyway; his patient was gone. Hank and Charley searched the place and ended up out back because the alley-way door was ajar.

Charley pointed northward. "The liverybarn sure as hell."

He was correct. When they arrived in the yard up there Walt Ridgeway was soaping harness in a shady place and told them that Hatfield had ridden out no more than fifteen minutes earlier.

"He didn't say nothing, just that he wanted his horse rigged out. That was all. By golly he looked real good considerin' all that happened to him a short while ago."

Hank led the way back to the roadway for a brief palaver. Charley was all for riding to the Hatfield place immediately, before Hatfield had the opportunity to put his personal things

together and leave. Hank was perfectly agreeable, but, as he said, they couldn't go off without
making some preparations for their prisoners to
be cared for.

Charley returned to the yard to get Ridgeway to
lend him a hand at rigging out their animals,
while Hank loped down to the café to see if the
caféman would feed and water the prisoners. The
caféman listened to all Hank had to say, then put
a sulphurous look upon Trainer as he said, "Give
me one damned reason why I should do a favor
for you or your partner. Just one. And do you
know what's goin' to happen when old Balinger
hears about you killin' two of his men and
lockin' up the others? He'll have you blown to
Kingdom Come. I don't think I want to be
involved."

"What about your brother?" asked Hank, and
the caféman, who had been turning away, turned
slowly back. "What about him," he growled.
"You think usin' that will get me to do you a
favor? Guess again, lawman."

Hank straightened up off the counter where he
had been leaning. "Next time I see you, mister, I
might have some information for you about your
brother."

The caféman's expression turned sourly skeptical. "Might have."

Hank did not reply. They stood gazing at each
other for a few moments, then Hank turned to

116

depart, and the caféman allowed him to reach the door before he said, "Where are the damned keys?"

Hank half smiled. "On the desk, right where your brother left them—and friend—be careful; don't let them out."

The caféman looked as though he might say something disagreeable, so Hank threw him a wave and walked back out where the sunsmash was more noticeable now than it had been earlier.

Charley was waiting with the horses. They left Parral by the upper stageroad and loped for a short distance, until they came to the right-hand turnoff, then dropped to a walk and said little as they studied fresh shod-horse marks going in the same direction.

Charley finally fished for his cut plug because the heat was drying his throat. After pouching a cud he said, "Balinger had Hatfield figured about right, only I don't think any of 'em down here knew just how big a swindler Hatfield really was."

Hank tipped down his hatbrim and peered ahead. By his estimate Jim Hatfield could not be more than a couple of miles ahead, maybe he was already at his ranch: but Doctor Gregg had specifically said Hatfield could not ride hard, and that was what he would be called upon to do if he saw the two federal deputy marshals coming so according to Hank's guess he and

Charley would be able to overtake Hatfield without much effort.

There was dust miles beyond the Hatfield place. A fairly big cloud of it, and it was moving on a diagonal course as though the men beneath it were aiming for town. Hank had a misgiving and voiced it. "Balinger. Someone slipped out of town sure as hell and dusted it out here to tell Balinger what happened. That'll be him and the rest of his crew."

They watched the distant tan banner without commenting for quite a while, each troubled with private thoughts about what was going to happen in town when a fighting-mad John Balinger roared into Parral with the balance of his rangemen. Charley thought it might be a good idea to abandon Hatfield and go back to Parral. Hank wavered, and in the end decided to let the caféman and anyone else in Parral who wanted to uphold the law do whatever was required of them, while the federal officers ran Jim Hatfield to earth.

He said, "Yonder's the barn." Moments later they had all the rooftops in sight, and there was dust up in the Hatfield yard too. Charley spat amber, straightened up in the saddle with squinted eyes fixed dead ahead, and said, "Just in case, we better keep the barn between us and the house."

That was what they did, left the road and began

angling toward the yard so that the old barn was in front of them all the way. Charley's jaws scarcely moved. He was watching the yard and structures up ahead to the exclusion of his cud of chewing tobacco. As long as he and his partner were riding in the direction of the yard, the only protection they had was the old barn, and if Hatfield happened to be inside it they would have no protection at all.

"He might not shoot," Hank muttered, also watching the rear of the barn intently.

Charley spat. "Might not. That'd make a right nice epitaph, wouldn't it? Carved in stone it would read nice, Hank: 'Here lies a damned idiot who thought he wouldn't shoot'."

Almost any other time Hank would have grinned to himself. This time he acted as though he had not heard Charley speak. They were within saddlegun range of the doorless rear barn opening. Their horses were slogging along, heads down, reins flopping, as though there was no peril within many miles.

They got still closer, almost within six-gun range, before one of the horses pricked up his ears a little and looked ahead.

But whatever held the horse's interest did not do as much for the other horse; he plodded right on up to the rear of the barn and only halted when his rider lifted a reinhand, then stepped to the ground. If Hatfield was inside the barn, he had just missed the finest opportunity to eliminate a pair of federal lawman he would ever have.

Hank and Charley palmed their six-guns and led their horses into the barn, where it was fifteen degrees cooler, and did not encounter a soul. Not even the flies which ordinarily hid from searing heat inside cool old barns.

Twelve
Trainer's Surprise

There was no sign of anyone over at the house, but then except for a horse out front, there probably would not have been anyway if Hatfield was inside.

It was the lack of a saddled horse out front which bothered Charley until Hank said Hatfield might have tethered his animal out back.

Because the house, as with most ranch houses, was fairly distant from the barn, with a lot of open yard separating them, there was no way to leave the barn on the way across to the house without being seen, providing someone inside the house was watching.

It was not Hank's idea to tempt the fates by stepping out into plain sight. He was not sure Hatfield would shoot; as far as he and Charley knew, Jim Hatfield had no serious reason to suspect the federal lawmen were after him. On the other hand Hatfield would not be the first man whose conscience saw everyone with a badge as a mortal enemy.

Charley reconnoitered out back and decided there was a way to flank the house along the west side by utilizing the outbuildings which were strung out on that side of the yard between the house and barn. There were wide gaps between but Charley could afford to be philosophical about that; as he told Hank, it was still better than trying a frontal approach across the yard from the barn, in plain sight all the way.

They left the barn by the same opening they had used to enter it, and turned to their left. The first outbuilding was a long-unused bunkhouse, half squared logs, half adobe. They got over behind it without difficulty, and remained over there for a while peering ahead in the direction of a thick-walled smokehouse where meat had once been cured. Although the squarely functional, ugly little building had not been used in many years, when the sun hit directly upon it it was still possible to catch a faint scent of cure.

Charley sank to one knee, removed his hat and peered around the corner of the thick-walled building. The house was as silent and as empty-seeming as ever. He was wagging his head when he pulled back and said, "I got a feelin' he's not over there."

Five seconds later they distinctly heard a door slam somewhere inside the house. Hank looked down at his partner. "The Mexes call 'em *fantasmas*."

Charley ignored that and got up to his feet and dusted his britches.

They had several yards of open territory to cross to reach the next outbuilding, which was a three-sided blacksmithing shed, with soot on the ceiling and the walls, and everything else in there.

Hank sent Charley first, and remained behind to cover for him. But nothing happened. Then Charley watched the house while Hank loped ahead, got inside the shoeing-shed and made the mistake of placing a palm against an upright when he leaned to look around. The hand came away as black as Tobie's hind-end, and Hank swore under his breath as he sought—and found—the customary water bucket and cleaned his hand.

Charley hissed and Hank went forward drying the hand down one side of his britches.

Someone was in the parlor over yonder making noise. They could not see him, but whatever he was doing had him engrossed at it; he was banging drawers, or cupboards, everything he opened and closed, and he was doing it rapidly.

Hank looked around and jerked his head. They were reckless this time, but the alternative was not much better; from the shoeing-shed to the main-house the distance was possibly fifty yards, and whether they tried to make the crossing from out back, or directly toward the porch from the front of the shoeing-shed, the distance and lack of protective cover was about the same.

Hank fisted his six-gun as he broke clear and started to run. Charley was a short distance to the rear, and was also holding his handgun as he ran.

Nothing happened. They made it to the porch, halted, scarcely breathed as they stepped onto wooden planking, and exactly what they feared and had hoped would not occur happened—the boards protested under their weight and the noise was loud enough to carry a fair distance.

Inside, those other sounds suddenly ceased.

Hank pressed close to the front of the house. It was the only shelter, and it did not make either Hank or his partner feel particularly secure.

Hank leaned. There was a window along the front wall close at hand. He could only have seen through it, inside, by exposing his upper body which he did not do. He had not really expected to be able to see inside, that had not been his intention. He called out.

"Hatfield! This it Federal Marshal Hank Trainer. My partner and I would like to talk to you."

For a long moment there was absolute silence, then the man inside the house called back, "I thought Balinger's foreman killed you. That's what someone said at the liverybarn in town."

Hank's retort was dry. "Well, Mister Hatfield, no one's told me yet so I'm still standing up, and I'd like a few words with you."

"What about?"

"Things in general."

The silence returned and continued for so long

Hank and Charley did not believe Hatfield was going to answer, so Hank spoke again. "What you heard in town was backwards—Balinger's foreman was the one who got killed, it wasn't either of us."

That got a response. "Frank Cartwright? I don't believe it. Who killed him?"

"Well, that don't matter right now, Mister Hatfield. What matters is that he is dead, and we want to talk to you, and if you won't come out we'll have to come in. It's up to you."

"Did one of you fellers kill Frank Cartwright?"

"Yes."

"I'm coming out. You hear me, Marshal? I'm coming out and I don't have a gun. You hear me?"

"We hear you, Mister Hatfield."

"No guns, Marshal. No shooting and no guns."

"There won't be any shooting, Mister Hatfield, if you walk out of there with empty hands."

The door opened but for a long while no one stepped through, and Charley was muttering under his breath with exasperation, then Hatfield walked out upon the porch and turned, facing the federal officers. He seemed not to be breathing. He flopped both arms. "Unarmed, gents. No weapons."

He was clearly afraid. Hank and Charley watched him, then Charley signaled for him to walk over to the railing at the edge of the porch, which he did, and Charley holstered his weapon, hooked both thumbs in his belt and solemnly regarded this man for whom he had never felt anything at all—neither hostility nor liking, and certainly no respect.

Hank felt the same, but showed it less as he said, "We didn't expect you'd be able to leave town for a few days yet."

The calmness of Hank's conversational tone of voice seemed to relax Hatfield. "Gregg said I could leave. Just nothing strenuous for a while." He gazed from Hank to Charley, and back. "Sure as hell you left town before John Balinger heard about the killin' of his rangeboss. If I was in your boots, I wouldn't be standin' here right now, I'd be making fast tracks out of the country."

Charley said, "Yeah, we're fixin' to leave, Mister Hatfield. First, though, we'd like you to explain to us about all the money you made peddlin' shares in those caches of your grandpappy which don't exist any more than he does."

Hatfield considered Charley Rivers; his expression suggested that he had something to say but was not quite sure that saying it would not anger Charley, and as had happened other times during the partnership of Rivers and Trainer, people had surmised that Charley was more likely to have a bad temper than Hank was.

Finally, Hatfield took a chance. "It don't concern you fellers. I didn't break any federal laws.

126

In fact, I didn't break any laws at all. I got a right to sell shares."

"Not if you knew there was no cache," stated Hank.

Hatfield was getting bolder. "Can you prove there wasn't none?"

Hank smiled slightly. "No, I sure can't."

Hatfield also smiled. His expression was that of a predator. "Then for all you know there is a cache."

"Not in the old gent's coffin, because we dug down and opened it. There was nothing in the box but the old gent and the blankets they'd wrapped him in."

Shock showed on Hatfield's face as Hank paused before continuing to speak.

"But there's something else, Mister Hatfield. We do have authority to lock folks up for murder."

This time even Charley looked shocked. "When the town marshal from Parral came out here, you steered him toward the gravesite, then you rode around, got ahead, set up an ambush, and when he came plodding along you blew him out of the saddle. We can prove it, Mister Hatfield. That's why we came out here after you left town. Not because you been working a swindler's game on folks like Joe Gregg. You're dead right, we got no authority to nail your hide for that. But murder is different. Raise your coat,

Mister Hatfield. I know you said you weren't armed, but in my book an ambush-killer isn't to be trusted no matter what he says. Hold your coat out!"

Hatfield moved almost automatically to hold his coat open. There was no weapon beneath. He let the coat fall and started to speak, but Charley, less trusting than his partner, ordered Hatfield to stand up and raise both arms. Then Charley made a thorough search—and came up with a bootknife and one of those little nickel-plated under-and-over .41 derringers which fit perfectly into a small arm-holster. The belly-gun had a pair of two-inch barrels.

Charley turned toward Hank wearing a disgusted look, but Hank scarcely heeded the concealed weapons as he said, "We'll haul you back and let the folks of Parral decide what to do with you. Charley, watch him, I'm going inside and see what he was up to."

The moment Hank entered the house he heard a steady thumping sound and went out to the kitchen. The dog was able to stand; in fact, he was able to walk over to Hank and stand there looking up, tail wagging. He had eaten all the food they had left, and had finished all the water as well. Evidently Jim Hatfield had not been interested in his dog because he had not even refilled the water-pan. Hank took care of that, then rummaged a cupboard until he found a tin of meat, which he opened and emptied in the dog's dish, then he returned to the parlor where an open black satchel sat atop a table. Expecting it to contain shaving things, perhaps a change of attire, personal items Jim Hatfield had stuffed in it, he started past, toward the back of the house, then turned back to quickly look in.

The satchel, which was about the size of those leather valises doctors took with them when they made house calls, had neatly bundled sheaves of money in it, and atop the money was a loaded six-shooter.

Hank removed the weapon, counted the bundles, replaced them, put the six-shooter back atop them, closed the satchel and left it on the table while he went throughout the house.

Nothing seemed to have been disturbed in the other rooms, only in the parlor where someone had used a light pry-bar to work out a big stone from the side of the fireplace.

Hank returned to the porch and pitched the satchel to his partner. "Six thousand dollars in there, and a six-shooter. I guess Mister Hatfield didn't put it all in the bank like he told Joe Gregg he did." Hank faced Harkness's grandson, who was staring at the satchel. "Where's your horse?" He had to repeat it before Hatfield replied.

"Out back, tied in the shade of a cottonwood tree. That money in the satchel is legitimately mine."

Hank did not argue; he jerked his head and led the way down off the porch and around the side of the house. When they got to the dozing horse he unlooped the reins, snugged up the cincha, told Hatfield to lead the horse and head for the bars.

When they were midway across the yard he also said, "I hope it's legitimately yours, Mister Hatfield, because you're goin' to need one hell of a good lawyer to keep from gettin' hanged."

At the barn as they were preparing to mount their own animals and Charley was tying the satchel to his saddle, he said, "While you was inside, Hank, he kept asking how we could prove he bushwhacked the town marshal."

Charley was clearly asking for an explanation, too. Hank had not mentioned the bushwhacking at all, not once, on their ride out to the Hatfield place.

He did not mention it now as he led his horse out of the barn before stepping up. He simply jerked his head for Hatfield to line up between the federal lawmen, then set the course for Parral, without opening his mouth.

Thirteen
The Parral Jailhouse

It was a glum ride. By the time they reached town the heat was noticeable and the roadway had its share of traffic. People watched them ride by, eyes fixed on the pair of federal lawmen because by now the news had spread about the killings in the saloon.

At the jailhouse, while Hank was watching his latest prisoner empty everything into his hat, Charley went to stand by the window and carve off a fresh chew. When he turned to watch Hatfield, Hank said, "Figured we'd see Balinger out there when we got back," and Charley chewed and peered, then shrugged and continued to chew without commenting. But Hatfield had something to say.

"You're fools to stay here. You've never seen old Balinger when he's mad."

Charley sauntered over to take the cell-room keys from Hank and herded Hatfield across in the direction of the cell-room door. From over there Hatfield reiterated it. "He'll bury you both. You should have fled when you had the chance."

Charley went along with his prisoner, and up in the front office the roadside door opened to admit the dour caféman. "Saw you ride in," he told Hank. "I fed them cowboys. They're fit to be tied."

Hank eased back his hat and gazed at the caféman. "Have you seen Balinger and his riders in town today?"

The caféman had indeed seen them. "Yeah. You bet I saw 'em. And they saw me. Old Balinger ordered me to turn his men out."

"But you didn't."

"That's right. That old son of a bitch has been ridin' roughshod ever since I been in this country. I figured someday we'd tangle. Well—I told him I had the only key, wouldn't turn his men out, and he'd have to see you fellers."

"What did he say to that?"

"Nothing. He went out of the café, spoke a little with his men, then they all climbed astraddle and rode out of town. I worried because I figured they would go lookin' for you boys."

Hank built and lit a smoke. "We didn't see 'em. We came directly to town from the Hatfield place. Where you expect Balinger went?"

"Want me to guess?"

"Yeah."

"Cattlemen hang together. I'd guess he went out to round up some friends and then he'll come back, and someone will open them cells or he'll come in here shootin' and do it himself."

When he finished speaking the caféman looked steadily at Hank. "All right, Marshal, I bought in on the side of the law. What you got to tell me about the killin' of my brother?"

Hank trickled smoke. He did not have anything to report which he could support with truth, so he simply said, "I need a little more time. Maybe until the morning. All right?"

The caféman did not look particularly disappointed. He had probably thought Hank would come up with nothing, anyway. As he went to the door he said, "He's got three fellers with him, and they didn't look very friendly."

Hank leaned to stub out his smoke as he replied to that statement with a question. "Is one of them a tall, lanky man?"

The caféman nodded. "Yeah. His name's Chet something-or-other. He don't come to town as often as the other riders do." The caféman lingered a moment in the open doorway. "Marshal, we used to have a vigilante committee in Parral. Some of the fellers are still around. I can roust up a few if you figure the law might need a little help when Balinger comes back."

Hank smiled. "I got no authority to prohibit you folks in Parral from doing what you think's got to be done, but as far as I know, friend, vigilantes can be worse than outlaws."

The caféman said, "Not this bunch," and walked out into the sunshine closing the door after himself, and Hank watched his partner return from the cell-room looking irritable. As

Charley dropped the key-ring atop the desk and glanced up, he said, "The cowboys sure don't care much for Mister Hatfield."

Hank sat down at the desk. He did not much care for Mister Hatfield either. Charley went to look into a little blue graniteware coffee-pot atop the dusty old woodstove. He shook his head; the grounds in the pot had been mildewing for several weeks.

A visitor came through the roadside opening and smiled the same smile he had showed the lawmen when they had first arrived in Parral. Without preliminaries he said, "What in hell are you stayin' around for? Didn't no one tell you Mister Balinger was in town a while back?"

Charley and Hank eyed the liverybarn hostler named Ridgeway. He had been the first person in the Parral country to befriend them.

Hank said they knew Balinger had been through. He also said they were waiting for him now, and Walt Ridgeway rolled his eyes but kept silent. He clearly did not believe Rivers and Trainer had good sense. Eventually he said, "Doctor Gregg was up at the liverybarn a while back turnin' in his rig; he just got back from deliverin' a baby. He told us from the way he'd been told you fellers never give Frank Cartwright a chance."

Hank sighed. "We gave them both a chance."

The hostler seemed willing to accept this, but

he was of the opinion that Balinger would not believe it, and shortly before departing he made an offer. "I got a shack about eighteen miles northwest of here, in a brushy canyon. It's been used before for a hideout. I can draw you a map to it."

Hank was appreciative, but said he did not believe they would need the hideout, and the hostler left after standing a moment in the doorway looking at them as though he thought they were shy some marbles.

They went over to the café one at a time to eat, and with shadows puddling the tension in Parral had stretched about as far as it could. People had been remaining off the plankwalks for most of the afternoon. By early evening they were leaving their main thoroughfare to a few scavenging dogs and a pair of inebriated old gaffers who were arguing out front of the general store, while hanging onto the same upright post.

When the riders appeared it was from the west side of town, coming in at a dead walk, seven of them, each man armed with a booted Winchester and his belt-gun. Neither Charley nor Hank saw them because they came from the direction where there was no window in the jailhouse, but Walt Ridgeway opened the roadside door, poked his head in to announce the return of John Balinger with other stockmen, then ducked back out and closed the door.

Charley strolled to a front-wall, grilled window to peer out. There was as yet no sign of horsemen. He stood over there until he could hear them, then spoke over his shoulder. "Sounds like more'n a handful."

Hank crossed to the front wall to lean and look down the roadway, but he could not see far enough so he went back to the desk, perched upon a corner of it, still with his hat tipped back, and considered the old stove, the dusty gunrack, and finally the oaken cell-room door with its half ton of reinforcing steel and bolts. Whoever had created that door—and it did not look to be anywhere nearly as old as the rest of the building—had possessed a very strong feeling about outlaws, or jailbreaks, or had simply felt impelled to demonstrate how good he was at creating something like that. It was doubtful that dynamite could break the door, although it might rip loose the massive steel hinges which held it bolted to the west wall.

Charley interrupted his partner's reverie. "Now I can see 'em. Seven, an' loaded for bear, with Balinger and some other old cowman riding up front."

Hank went over to lean and look. He recognized only two of the horsemen, John Balinger and that tall cowboy who had painstakingly pared his fingernails at the bunkhouse when Balinger had spoken to Trainer and Rivers. He

no whiskey, not even tobacco because he did not use it, or if he did they did not ever remember having seen him do it.

But he probably would not have accepted anything. He crossed his legs, removed the hat and placed it upon an upraised knee, and said, "You know Balinger's in town. He's got Lewis Haley with him. Haley ranches west of Parral. He owns almost as much land and cattle as Mister Balinger, and they've always hung together, especially when there's been trouble."

Hank spread his arms. "There is no trouble. That was much earlier in the day. Balinger can have his riders back any time. If there was a town constable it'd be up to him, but since there isn't and we're the only lawmen around, and we can't act as township marshals, why then I expect he can have his men back—if the townfolk don't have something else in mind."

Doctor Gregg looked at Hank Trainer. "He said he figures to make a clean sweep when he comes over here—you boys on horseback heading out of the territory, escorted the first fifty miles by his riders, *after* we've held a court hearing about you two killing a pair of his men, and assuming you are acquitted—which I personally do not believe you will be—and after that he wants your other prisoner turned over to him."

Charley was angry. He turned on the medical man with fire in his eyes. "Who the hell does that old man think he is! You go tell him he don't dictate to the federal law. You tell that old son of a bitch if he thinks he can break his riders out of here with us inside, he's crazy."

Doctor Gregg turned disconsolately to face Hank, and all he got from that direction for a long time was a steady stare and not a sound. Then Hank said, "He's got a rider over yonder with him whose name is Chet something-or-other. You go tell Balinger we want to talk to Chet before we make any decisions."

The medical man leaned to arise. "He's not going to make compromises. I never knew Balinger very well, but I know him that well. He's worked very hard at being head honcho in the Parral countryside for many years. He's not going to accept some decision you men have made."

Hank said, "That'll be up to him, Doctor, not you."

Charley held the door until the medical man was half-way across the roadway, then Charley saw the caféman and several cronies watching everything from behind the cafe's fly-specked front window.

Charley beckoned, the caféman stepped to his doorway, and Charley told him they needed food for the prisoners and themselves.

The caféman remained in his doorway, arms crossed over his chest, gazing stonily at

Charley, toward whom he had no particular reason to be friendly. Then he abruptly turned, and when some of his cronies inside behind the front-wall window said something to him the caféman did not answer, but walked directly to his kitchen.

Charley closed and barred the door, saw Hank watching and said, "Did someone tell us that caféman's name?"

"Yeah. Glen Butler."

"Well, when all this mess is over with I'm goin' to catch hold of his collar and yank about a yard of slack out of him. I never got very fond of unsmilin' disagreeable sons of bitches, an' that's exactly what I'd call him. And I'll lay you ten to one he don't bring over any grub. I know his kind, Hank. Measly, snide, temperamental, vindictive an' downright mean."

Hank returned to a corner of the old desk, hitched himself up into a sitting position, and went to work manufacturing another smoke. Ordinarily he was not that heavy a smoker, but these were troublesome times.

Ten minutes later when someone snarled for the door to be opened, and the caféman entered loaded with trays and lidded coffee-tins, Hank gazed amusedly at his partner.

Charley got a little rusty colored in the face, and he stammered when the caféman placed their food atop the desk, then turned to depart.

Charley saw the look he was getting from Hank, understood perfectly what his partner was thinking, and nearly choked when he thanked the caféman and saw him to the door.

Fourteen
End of the Trail

Charley fed the prisoners and Hank remained up in the office watching the roadway. Shadows had settled; it was not dark yet, but it was dusky out, still warm, rather pleasant, even for the men Hank watched stroll from the saloon down to the café. Charley had said there were seven of them. With Balinger there were eight, and this time as they strolled upon the opposite side of the road they frankly eyed the dark, fortress-like old adobe jailhouse.

When Charley returned wagging his head over the complaints of the prisoners, he and Hank hauled chairs to the old desk and also ate.

Hank said, "It won't be long. Maybe an hour."

Charley was not too worried. "Balinger hires some ornery riders. I never before been threatened so many different ways by a cell full of prisoners."

They had finished eating, had retrieved and stacked the tinware and utensils from the cell-room, and were swilling the last of their coffee when a tall, gangling man pushed in from the roadway and stood blinking because of the gloom.

Both Trainer and Rivers recognized him at

once. He had been inside Balinger's bunkhouse with them, as silent and aloof as a stone.

Charley went after the lamp to create more light, and ignored their visitor while Hank pointed to a chair and replied when the rangeman asked why they wanted to see him, and Hank was blunt about it. "You were the guard up yonder where those redrock spires are—by the Harkness grave?"

The gangling man sat down and shoved out very long legs before answering. He seemed perfectly at ease as he watched Charley hang the office lamp from a hook in the ceiling.

"You already know that," the tall man replied indifferently, still watching Charley. "It was mentioned when you was at the ranch with Mister Balinger. What about it?"

"You saw Hatfield bushwhack the town marshal," Hank said.

The gangling man's head came around and his eyes widened upon Hank. "What the hell are you trying to do?" he growled. "That town marshal was ambushed several miles south of where I was keepin' watch."

Hank smiled at the gangling man. "Naw, mister; you were ridin' south for a little exercise, and saw the marshal ridin' north, and about the time you thought you might change course and palaver with him for a spell you saw someone rise up behind some brush and shoot the town marshal off his horse."

144

The tall man frowned at Hank. "You're crazy, mister."

Charley finished with the lamp and strolled toward the door. At the very last minute he whirled and pushed a six-gun into the tall man's face, and cocked it.

Hank spoke again. "Chet, I'm satisfied about who killed the town marshal, and I think I know why he killed him, but what I got to have is some proof, and you're goin' to provide it."

Charley straightened up, eased down the hammer of his Colt and holstered the weapon, and looked at the gangling man with an expression of unalloyed hostility. Charley did not know what Hank was doing, but he was willing to back him in it, as he had done upon other occasions. He genuinely did not care for the tall cowboy. That feeling went back to when the tall man stood guard over Charley and Hank at the Balinger bunkhouse; at that time the tall man had looked with frank contempt upon Trainer and Rivers.

Chet read Charley's face without effort, and avoided looking at it as he said, "Who bushwhacked the town marshal?"

Hank did not hesitate. "Jim Hatfield. I'm as satisfied about that as I am that I'm talkin' to you right now."

"Why would he do that?"

"I got a hunch, but I really don't know. So

Charley's going to fetch him up here in the front office, and in his presence you're going to tell me that you were ridin' south from the redrock area, saw the killing, and turned off toward the home-place to report it to Mister Balinger."

Chet continued to regard Hank Trainer with a look of doubt on his face. "All right. But I'll lay you odds it don't work."

Hank was not sure it would work either, but as he had explained, he could do nothing without a witness.

Then Chet had something else to say. "When I get back across the road, Mister Balinger's comin' over here with Mister Haley and their riders and take our riding crew out of here. I'll give you some advice but I doubt like hell that you'll take it. Anyone crazy enough to believe they can hoodwink Hatfield into admittin' he murdered someone isn't likely goin' to be sensible about somethin' else."

Hank was rolling a smoke when he said, "Fetch him up here, Charley," and as Rivers turned toward the cell-room door, Hank lit up, blew smoke at the taller man, and looked at him from eyes which showed icy and absolute determination, then he said, "Chet, you better turn into a real good actor. If you don't we're goin' to send you back across the road in pretty bad shape."

The gangling man looked away from Hank, considered the dingy walls, the fly-specked ceiling, the old rack along the west wall, and faced Trainer again only when he heard Charley gruffly telling someone to shut up.

Chet said, "They been tellin' Mister Balinger you fellers never give Frank nor our youngest rider a chance."

Hank did not respond, he instead twisted to watch Jim Hatfield emerge from the cell-room and pause to squint in the office light. When he recognized the gangling man his jaw muscles rippled. Otherwise he neither nodded nor spoke, and the gangling rangerider reacted in similar fashion. Clearly these two knew, and did not care much for, each other.

Charley herded Hatfield to a bench and watched him ease down, favoring his injured leg. Hank and Chet also eyed Harkness's grandson, allowing time to run on for a moment or two before Hank said, "You wanted to know what proof I had that you murdered the town marshal. There he sits; he saw you go into hiding and waited to see what you were up to, then he saw you shoot the constable off his horse. And he'll take an oath about what he saw."

Jim Hatfield leveled a glassy-eyed stare at the gangling man. He did not cry out a denunciation as Hank expected, he sat on his bench looking steadily at Chet. Finally, he said, "You didn't see anything. If you'd been anywhere around I'd have seen you."

Hank smiled. "You weren't watchin' for anyone but the town marshal. What I'd like to know is why—what did he do, or say to you when he stopped by the ranch, that made you decide to ambush him?"

Hatfield swung to eye Charley Rivers, who was leaning on one raised leg where his booted foot rested upon the same bench. Charley wagged his head. "Sure as I'm standin' here, *amigo*, they're goin' to hang you."

Hatfield looked scornful. "If anyone gets lynched it won't be me, it'll be the men who killed Frank Cartwright. Mister Balinger set a lot of store by him."

Chet arose and said, "Hatfield, if these fellers hang you're goin' to be right beside 'em. I saw you murder the constable and I'm goin' to volunteer as a witness to that among the townfolk." He stepped to the closed door to rest a hand upon the latch while he eyed Hank Trainer.

Hank nodded. "Go ahead," he told the gangling man. "Tell Mister Balinger we're lookin' forward to talkin' to him and any other feller he wants to bring along. But just one other, you understand?"

Chet lifted the latch at the same time he started to speak, but Hank raised a hand. "Just one other feller. No argument." He eyed Chet briefly, then crookedly smiled. "Thanks. I'll keep you posted."

Chet did not return the smile, instead he woodenly regarded Hank, Charley, and finally, Jim Hatfield, then he walked out and slammed the jailhouse door after himself.

Hank looked around. Hatfield was still looking at the roadway door when he said, "He's lyin' to you fellers. He didn't see anything."

Hank nodded at Charley, who nudged Hatfield up to his feet and took him back down into the cell-room. Moments later, as Charley was closing the oaken door at his back, John Balinger flung the roadside door inward and entered, followed by that taller older cowman named Lewis Haley. Balinger did not look violent; he did not look affable, but he did not seem to be as angry as Hank and Charley had been led to believe he was.

He introduced Haley, who solemnly nodded, then Balinger said, "I'll give you boys a choice. Turn out my riders or have this damned old adobe shack pulled down around your ears."

Charley was not impressed. "These are four-foot walls, Mister Balinger."

The cowman lifted his coat to disclose three tubes wrapped in red paper. "And these," he told Charley, "are sticks of dynamite." He dropped the coat, and Charley went to a bench, having nothing more to say. Balinger faced Hank Trainer. "We talked and you boys said you would leave the country."

That was true. Hank inclined his head. "We're

going, Mister Balinger. Did Chet talk to you after he left this office?"

He had. "Yes; you mean about your idea to get Hatfield to admit to murder? It won't work. You don't know Hatfield. He's a treacherous, devious son of a bitch but he's not a fool. They'd lynch him sure as hell, right here in town. That constable was pretty well liked."

Hank considered the cowman, and brought up the topic Balinger surely would have brought up shortly. "Your rangeboss was abusive. He was spoilin' for a fight. The barman and anyone else who was in the bar at the time could tell you that. But the best witnesses are my prisoners. If you want, you can leave your weapons here on the desk then go down there and ask them what happened without Charley or me going along. It sure as hell wasn't murder, and it sure as hell wasn't us who started it."

Balinger seemed to be thinking; he said nothing for a long while, then turned to glance at Lewis Haley. The larger cowman gravely inclined his head. He believed Hank's suggestion was a good one.

Balinger went to the cell-room door, did not go near the desk, but when Charley Rivers stepped up, Balinger lifted out his six-gun, handed it to Charley, then ignored them all as he swung back the oaken door and went down the dingy corridor beyond.

Hank pointed to a chair for Lewis Haley, who went to it and sat down eyeing Hank Trainer. Lewis Haley did not act like a person who talked a lot, and he wasn't. He watched Hank build a smoke, watched Charley skive off a cud, and eventually said, "Can you prove you're federal deputies?"

They showed him their badges, and Hank got the impression he was not convinced. They did not carry any other identification, and actually, Hank did not particularly care what Lewis Haley believed.

The cowman looked around, then said, "I knew the constable right well. In fact, some years back he rode for me. That was before he put in for the lawman's job."

Hank and Charley sat in silence, waiting for whatever came next. It was a long wait. Not only was Lewis Haley reticent, he also said things in his own good time, and in his own particular way.

"Fact is, gents, when he quit to come to Parral an' be their lawman, I give him a six-gun. It was almost new. I'd had it six, seven years. Won it right here in town in a poker session."

Hank turned and caught Charley looking at him. Hank nodded, and Charley went to the corner where Hatfield's bullion satchel stood, brought the satchel to the desk, opened it, dug out the six-gun and handed it to Lewis Haley.

"You ever see this one before?" he asked. "Hatfield had a separate gun on him when we brought him in. That there gun was inside his money satchel."

Haley turned the gun over several times, hefted it, even ascertained by an arm's-length hold that the gun was loaded. Then he turned up the butt plate, looked at it for a long time, and finally twisted to pitch the weapon atop the desk.

"That's it," he said. "I could identify the little star scratched on the bottom of the butt plate, and some other markings on it. That's the gun I gave the town marshal, and that's the gun he carried from the day he taken the oath of his office to the day he died." For a while Haley had no more to say, his long, expressionless, weathered and bronzed features impassive and grave. Then he finally said, "All right. You expect to trick Hatfield into a confession by using Chet as a witness to somethin' he didn't see. I'll tell you something; you don't need Chet. If that satchel with the gun and money in it belongs to Hatfield—the only way anyone could ever get that gun off the constable would be to kill him an' take it off his body. And you're absolutely positive that there satchel belongs to Jim Hatfield?"

Charley went into considerable detail to explain about the satchel, where they had got it from whom, which residence it had been in, and why he and his partner had been skulking around out at the Hatfield place.

Haley was a good listener. When he had heard it all he arose saying he'd like a word with Balinger, and went down into the cell-room. Charley scowled disapproval; Haley had still been armed. Charley stood in the doorway where he could see down there, and Hank replaced the gun in the satchel and put the satchel upon the floor behind the desk and chair he was using. Then he yawned.

Balinger returned to the office trailed by Lewis Haley. He shouldered past Charley, who was still standing at the cell-room door, and approached Hank Trainer. "You got Hatfield dead to rights," he said. "Lewis, here, just told Hatfield and me about the gun from Hatfield's satchel. You did a good job in Parral, Marshal."

Hank and Charley watched the cowman in silence. Balinger was not smiling.

"And you shot two of my men," Balinger stated.

Charley growled an answer to that. "Mister, I got no use for a man who'll beat an' kick a dog. That's for openers. That big son of a bitch picked the fight, we didn't. I'll tell you somethin' else, mister; anyone who'd hire a man like that don't get any respect from me either. You bet your boots I shot him. If he was standin' here now and

153

got to pushin' for a fight, I'd shoot him again. I don't care what you believe, mister—I shot Cartwright fair and square. You can ask those men of yours in the cells, but like I said, I don't give a damn what you believe."

Charley finished with a snarl, and Hank, who knew his partner very well, broke in to silence Charley before there was a fight. Hank said, "What did your riders tell you, Mister Balinger; that it was a fair fight or not?"

Balinger turned his back on Charley, who had angered him. "Fair—except that my rangeboss was no match for your partner."

Hank shrugged that off. "If he'd asked I could have told him that. Cartwright was a man who wouldn't ask, and wouldn't listen. Every grave-yard I've ridden past, Mister Balinger, has at least one fool like Cartwright in it. As for that younger feller—he had to draw. He had to prove he was a genuine rangeman. A lot of graveyards got a lot like that in them too. I'm sorry about him, but there was no choice."

Lewis Haley cleared his throat, went to peer into the little blue graniteware coffee-pot, then went back by the front wall to lean down and look across the road where his riders were slouching with Balinger's rangemen. While he was bent down like that he drily said, "John, take the key. It's there on the desk. Go let your fellers out. There's folks lookin' out of windows up an' down the roadway. That's all you got to do. You come in here an' by yourself freed your riders." Haley straightened up and turned. "That's all you got to do. Folks will see that. You'll be as respected as always."

Haley turned pale, steady eyes toward the desk where Hank was sitting. "You got any objections, Marshal?"

Hank saw John Balinger watching him. He picked up the brass ring of keys and pitched out where Balinger caught it. "No objections at all. We're ready to leave this country before tomorrow; I just want to know one thing. Who's goin' to be responsible for Jim Hatfield?"

Balinger was holding the ring of keys and seemed about to commit himself, when Lewis Haley spoke first. "I'll be responsible. I'll serve as lawman until we can hire another one, and I'll write up north for a circuit-ridin' judge to come down an' try Hatfield. But I'm not goin' to let Chet or anyone else testify that didn't see anything or wasn't around when the bushwhackin' happened."

Hank was agreeable to that. If he had known about that weapon in Hatfield's satchel, where the defunct lawman had got it and how, he would not have tried his bluff using Chet to intimidate Hatfield. But he had not known about the gun until about an hour ago.

He arose looking straight at John Balinger.

There was nothing to say. Balinger would never change. He had been as he was for more years than Hank or Charley had been alive. He would be the same way right up to the day they patted him in the face with a shovel.

Charley preceded Hank out of the jailhouse. Behind them, inside, Haley picked up the satchel, opened it, and showed Balinger the six-gun. Then he explained to Balinger how the murdered lawman had acquired that weapon, and when Balinger nodded his head while idly twirling the brass key-ring, Lewis Haley said, "John, I got to tell you something. In a way you harassed Hatfield into doin' some of the things he did. Next time you get into trouble, don't come lookin' for me. We'll go on working cattle together, and bein' friends, but there's a part of your nature I don't much care for. Better go let them boys out, they're most likely hungry as hell. I know I am."

So were Charley and Hank, but they turned their backs on the café, and as the hostler at the liverybarn got their animals then went after their outfits, Hank leaned on the tie-rack gazing out through the corralyard's sagging wide gates and wagged his head.

"You want to know something, Charley? I've yet to come down to the south desert country that I don't get involved in somethin' I had no inkling about."

Charley was carving a corner off his depleted plug of Kentucky twist. "You want to know something, Hank? I never yet been sent out with you that I ain't had to go hungry, get folks mad at me, get shot at, cussed out, sometimes jumped on—an' missed eatin' now and then."

When the hostler brought forth their outfits they relieved him of the chore of saddling up, did the job themselves, flipped him some silver coins, swung up and turned up out of Parral with moonlight and starshine to guide them. They knew by instinct how to get back up out of this country, and as long as the night was bland and fragrant they continued to ride.

They missed seeing the red dust, the redstone plinths, even the gravelly earth underfoot which was also mottled by streaks of rusty red soil.

They had to ride a fair distance before encountering a crooked roadbed, which they turned up, and as Hank looped his reins to make a smoke and light it, Charley said, "I guess I should have climbed down in and also looked at that face in the coffin. I got to write a report about Harkness."

Hank trailed smoke as he unlooped his reins and straightened up in the saddle. "Take my word for it. I'm pretty sure it was Pete Harkness."

Charley's head swung. "Pretty sure! You called up to me that it was him, for a fact."

Hank laughed. "Yeah. It was."

"Then why the hell did you just now say you was pretty sure?"

"Just to keep you awake. There's no water to camp by for another eight or ten miles."

Charley continued to glower, then he spat and straightened ahead in the saddle, screwed up his face in thought for a short distance and finally said, "You ever think about retiring, Hank?"

"Sure. Every now and then. Except that a man's got to earn wages to live on."

Charley sprayed amber again before speaking. "Unless he's got enough brains to get somethin' laid by."

Hank looked at his companion. "Who the hell can afford to do that on the kind of wages we earn?"

Charley ruminated for a while before saying, "Well, I been figurin' on retirin' pretty soon."

Hank scowled. "You never saved anything in your life, Charley."

Rivers smiled and patted his shirt-front. "A man don't always have to save it, Hank."

Hank rode a long while in silence. His cigarette went out while he stared intently at the man riding beside him. "What are you talkin' about, Charley?"

"You recollect all that money piled in stacks in that little satchel back yonder?"

Hank yanked his horse to a dead stop. "Charley, you didn't do any such a blamed

158

thing—did you? Charley, for Chris'sake, why did you tell me? I don't want to know anything like that."

Rivers turned, smiling a little in the warm moonlight. "Naw, I didn't do it, Hank. I just wanted to be sure you'd stay awake until we got up yonder where that water is so's we can camp."

They rode in silence for a dozen or so yards before Hank shook his head and blew out a big sigh of disgust and resignation. He should have expected it. Every time he pulled a trick on Charley, regardless of how long it took, Charley would figure out something to do in retaliation.

He suddenly ruefully laughed. Charley looked over and also laughed.

Center Point Publishing
600 Brooks Road ● PO Box 1
Thorndike ME 04986-0001 USA

(207) 568-3717

US & Canada:
1 800 929-9108
www.centerpointlargeprint.com